BACK TO THE SURFACE

And other stories

`

DAN CHIMSKY

This book is a work of fiction. Names, characters, places, and incidents either are products of the author's imagination or are used fictitiously. Any resemblance to actual events or locales or persons, living or dead, is entirely coincidental.

ISBN 978-1-7781101-2-2
ISBN 978-1-7781101-3-9 (eBook)

Mystery Woman

Dan Chimsky

Sarath could not focus on his work. His office, usually a neat, well-kept place, was full of stuff extracted from downstairs. His table was a total mess. And the whole building was stinky like a marshland. Suddenly, he heard a commotion among his staff, who were cleaning up the main floor.

"Sir, Sarath sir… come here quick," one of the workers yelled. His agitated voice was clearly a signal of something terribly wrong. Several others started to call him, too.

"Sir, there is another body. You should look this."

"Shit…, another one," Sarath muttered to himself. And rushed towards the staircase.

Seven days ago, the country saw the biggest natural disaster it had experienced in its entire history. The tsunami started in Indonesia, traveled across the Indian Ocean, and reached the African coast. On its way, the massive waves destroyed many nations, including Sri Lanka.

For the whole last week, everything was in chaos. The entire coastal region was without electricity and water supply. There were dead bodies, swollen and disfigured, still on the roadsides. The armed forces and volunteers have been working hard to bring back normalcy. But it was next to impossible due to the massive destruction in every direction.

The impact on Sarath's business was yet to be determined. His main office and store, a four-story building, was right next to the beach. And was hit hardest by the massive waves. But Sarath had to wait a week to start cleanup work in his place. Mainly because he couldn't find enough people. As the biggest wholesale store in the city, it needs more than the usual workforce under its fold.

Sarath requested his staff, only those not affected by the disaster, to come and start cleaning up. Three of his workers lost their close relatives to the waves. Four others had family members with various types of injuries. Although the remaining few members were not enough, he needed to start from somewhere.

Sarath quickly ran down the stairs. Everyone was gathered at the back end of the storage area. Farther back in the building. Hearing his footsteps, a few men moved to allow their boss. Even before getting a clear view, Sarath knew this was different. Among water-logged cardboard boxes, there was a dead body. A woman.

A few hours ago, they found another dead body in the building. Bloated and partially decomposed. And with an unbearable smell. But this one was entirely distinct. A miraculously preserved perfect living specimen. More importantly, it is of a foreign woman. Sarath could not believe his eyes. The young lady, probably in her early thirties, was sitting on a box. The jeans and white T-shirt were dry. Her neck was slightly bent towards the chest. One would think she is having a nap. But definitely not under these circumstances.

The others were staring at her in awe. Sarath understood their curiosity. Even he couldn't imagine whether the woman was still alive or dead. But the answer is clear. No one would survive after this many days.

Everyone gathered had seen far too many deaths in the past few days. And they all saw the body found in the store earlier. It was swollen and disfigured beyond recognition. Peeled-off skin added horror to the scene. Not a pleasant view by any means. But this was quite the opposite.

"Sir, what do we do now?" asked one staffer. Sarath reluctantly took his eyes off the beautiful face and looked at the back wall.

White plaster was smudged with brownish mud. A thick, dark brown line just a foot below the ceiling marked the water level that arose after the tsunami waves. Luckily, no one was at the store when the waves swept across the building. It was the Sunday after Christmas.

Sarath turned around and looked across the floor at the road. All glass panels in the front were gone. An eighteen-foot bus was struck inside the store. One floated through the glass panels with the destructive waves. City officials helped to drag it out two days ago.

Usually, a large section of the ground floor is full of boxes ready to be shipped to outstations. After the waves, everything was piled up against the back wall in total disarray. Sarath could not still assess the loss he incurred. But there are more urgent works to handle right now.

"I will call the police," said Sarath. He started to dial his cell phone while walking away from the group. "Guys... don't touch the woman."

With their boss out of sight, the conversation started again.

"I wonder how this one was not noticed before," said one of the workers. Rescue teams searched most of the hard-hit areas of the city for dead and injured for the past few days. The buildings closest to the beach got special attention. And shops like Sarath's were looted by some during the chaos. The robbers had gone through every possible place at night.

"People must have overlooked this under all these boxes," said another, looking at the pile behind.

"Yes... No one would see it under this mountain... not even looters."

"She must be a tourist. Poor girl...," an elder one sympathized.

"You know what? I don't think she was caught by the waves. How come her body moved this far? And under that pile of heavy boxes. I think someone had killed her last night. And dumped her body here," the youngest of the group speculated. A few others nodded in agreement. "Look at her body. You saw the other one in the morning. And bodies on the streets. This is not disgusting like those. Look how fresh her skin is."

"But there are no injuries on her body. No blood or anything like that," another one suggested. "If she was killed, how?"

"Maybe on her back. Or maybe poisoned... Who knows?" Another one suggested.

"Agree. See... there is no jewelry on the body. Not even a ring. Must have been stolen."

"Don't think so. This was buried at the bottom of this pile. How many boxes did we pull before seeing her body?"

"Don't you remember? We found the other one on top of this pile. Definitely, she was floated with the waves."

The discussion continued. No one wanted to move away from the beautiful woman. Even she was dead.

"Poor young lady... died here, thousands of miles away from her home. When the time is right, everyone should go." The eldest of the workers said. "We'll clear that side until the police come. Otherwise, the boss will be mad at us."

#

"Sir, we've got some intel," said Major Alwis, a Sri Lankan-born US citizen specially assigned for this mission. As he speaks the local language and is familiar with the island's culture, he was airlifted from Afghanistan. Within a few hours, he joined the special mission in the Indian Ocean.

"Go ahead," said General McMaster.

As this was not a combat operation, everyone was at ease. Some even considered it as a vacation. But it was a perfect training mission for the US Marines.

Four days ago, the US Marine Corps deployed five hundred personnel in southern Sri Lanka to assist in the humanitarian mission. Later, they distributed themselves and camped in four different areas that were hard hit by the tsunami.

The main camp, a closed public school, was busy with activity. They had more than expected observers outside the school fence. Locals were more interested in seeing unfamiliar vehicles like Humvees and various equipment in the school playground.

"Sir, a dead body of a foreign woman was found in a warehouse this morning," Major Alwis reported.

"Is she a US citizen?"

"Sir, the ID was not confirmed. No documents were found with the body. The local police hauled it to the hospital," the major hesitated a little. "There's another thing, Sir."

"What is it?"

"Locals have seen the body. It was not decomposed as the others died from the tsunami."

"Homicide?"

"Most probably, Sir."

"Go to the mortuary immediately. Take the MO with you." General stood from his chair. "I will stop by the police station on my way."

As Major Alwis saluted to leave, they heard a knock on the open door. The radio chief entered the room in a hurry.

"Yes?"

"Sir, you have incoming communication from the Pentagon in five minutes."

"Great, what now?... That ain't be good." General murmured to himself. "Okay, Let's go there." General walked towards the door with his subordinates.

"Major... On your way back, go to that warehouse. See if you can find anything to ID the body."

"Yes, Sir."

General McMaster followed the staff sergeant to the communication room, thinking about what the Pentagon needed now. One of the few walled classrooms was converted to accommodate expensive equipment. As they entered the room, other officers stood from their seats to salute the General. It didn't take long to receive the call from the Pentagon.

"General Collin McMaster... connecting to the CMC now," said the female voice on the other side.

This must be serious, McMaster thought. *Otherwise, the commandant wouldn't worry and call this late in the US*. It should be close to midnight there.

"General..., this is urgent. We've lost communication with a Sub close to your location. It was stationed in the Indian Ocean, east of Sri Lanka. All our efforts to connect with the sub failed. We had an important asset there. We don't want anyone to see that," the CMC explained.

"The last communication was four hundred miles east of the island, just before the waves hit that area. Don't think it was affected by the tsunami. There's no reason to believe it was close to the surface. We need to retrieve anything that survived at all costs. Understood?"

"Yes, Sir," said the general, thinking about what they'd been doing for seven days. If the nuclear submarine was lost a week ago, why wait this long to act?

"A second ESG is on its way to the Indian Ocean. You have enough air power to retrieve everything surfaces. Keep an eye on the east coast as well. If you need anything else, contact me right away," the commandant said.

A second Expeditionary Strike Group with three assault ships and a fleet of fighter jets and helicopters means this is serious business.

"Coordinate with General Scott immediately. He is in Australian waters right now. Update me in two hours," said the commandant.

#

The hospital was overcrowded with people. There were thousands of injured in the wards. Not everyone had beds. Many were on the floor waiting for their treatments. The relatives who came to visit them crammed the hospital grounds. Doctors and nurses struggled to provide necessary treatments with limited supplies. There was chaos everywhere.

For the moment, the hospital mortuary was relatively calm. However, it was stuffed inside with the dead. There were hundreds on the floor. Many are not even human-shaped anymore, swollen to unimaginable proportions. After several days of indecision, the government decided to perform mass burials.

At this time, most had given up finding their loved ones. The bodies were heavily disfigured after seven days. Therefore, identification was difficult for even the closest relatives. Most had lost clothes when fighting the waves. Usually, jewelry is a perfect way to recognize the owner by their close ones. But dead bodies had been thoroughly scanned by looters.

It was relatively peaceful at the morgue. After the three discharges in the morning, there have been no activities in the building. Nimal, the only one living at the facility, was sitting at the front desk, expecting to take a break. As the morgue attendant, he had the busiest work period for the last few days. For six days in a row, he's been working overtime. Through the glass window, he saw a man hurrying towards him. The owner of a funeral home, Samson.

"I got the news. What is it? Is it good?" the young man asked, even before he reached the desk.

"You are a fucking moron. Don't you have any sense?" asked Nimal.

"Is that true? Is it a foreigner?" Samson asked with a big smile. "If it is a white girl, we can sell it for a big sum," he placed his hand on the shirt pocket. A thick bundle of cash was visible across the thin white fabric.

"I heard it was not killed by the waves. It should be fresh. Isn't it? Man, show me the thing." He looked at the inner door impatiently.

"Who knows what? The cops will come again. They will do a post-mortem. We are waiting for the coroner," said the attendant, staring through the window.

"He's dead. I've just got the news this morning. He was on the train caught by the waves. Not even his body was found."

"Is that true? The poor guy."

"Don't think they can find another coroner for days in this situation. So, no more post-mortems."

"Yesterday, we buried five tractor loads. All remaining bodies will be sent to the cemetery tonight," said Nimal, shaking his head. "She'll have to go to the big dump with others... if there's no examination."

"That's more than enough time," Samson took a bundle of notes from his pocket. And passed it to the attendant without counting. He quickly pocketed it while looking around. No one was around except the dead across the wall.

Samson slipped through the inner door. It was a familiar place for the man in the white sarong. But it was not the usual sight inside. Dead bodies were arranged in rows along the walls. Touching each other. Samson ignored the horror. Under the dim light of the incandescent bulbs, he saw the metal table, his target, at the end of the chamber.

Samson grew up seeing the dead around him. He started to work at his father's funeral home at fourteen. Hence, never had a fear of corpses. He walked past the stinking piles of flesh and stopped at his target. The one on the table was distinct. He immediately recognized the freshness. No doubt, she was alive a few hours ago.

Samson stayed staring at the body, enjoying the beauty of this unknown woman. Her arms were on her sides. Long legs were parted slightly and reached the total length of the table. Her eyelids were firmly closed. Long eyelashes were intact. Short blond hair added an exotic beauty to her face. It was like a marble sculpture. He admired the creamy skin exposed in her arms and face. It was not dehydrated as in other corpses in the hall. He hesitantly touched the long, slender fingers of the right arm. Samson felt blood rushing to his groin. Blinded by the raging obsession, he failed to register the warmth of her skin.

Samson enjoyed every second of this encounter. Slowly, he raised the slender arm and kissed it. The skin felt fresh. No smell or dryness. He placed his right hand on the body. And slowly moved the white t-shirt to expose the belly. His hand gradually moved upward along the torso. He cupped one breast. It was firm, as in a young lass. He watched her face while fondling the breast under her bra. Then, moved the t-shirt and bra to further appreciate the naked beauty of the young woman. His eyes were transfixed on the perfect round shapes while his fingers squeezed the nipples.

What happened next was too swift to comprehend by any living human being.

In a quick movement, the woman sat on the table, throwing the man to the cement floor. It took a moment for him to realize what had happened. Frightened, he was staring at a pair of yellow-colored eyes. The woman jumped from the table and closed the gap. In a fraction of a second, he was kneeling on the ground. And was struggling to breathe. His nose was bleeding heavily. The woman adjusted her clothes and elegantly walked towards the door. Before she reached the door, Samson exhaled his last breath.

#

Nimal reluctantly finished the last cigarette he had. Smoking is prohibited on the hospital premises. Hence, he was at his usual hiding spot. A narrow alley between two buildings. The mortuary and the storerooms. He didn't want to disturb Samson while he was at his business.

When he turned the corner and faced the entrance, his joy evaporated. There were two visitors in front of the main door. Two giants in combat uniforms. He knew these were the American soldiers. Everyone in the town was aware of them these days.

"Brother... we need a little help," Major Alwis said in his mother tongue. Surprised by hearing his own dialect from the foreign soldier, Nimal quickened his steps.

"What's your name?" the major asked in a friendly manner. His hands were already on Nimal's shoulder.

"Nimal, Sir," the attendant answered hesitantly.

"I'm Major Alwis. This is our medical officer, Lieutenant Daniel Wadell," Major Alwis introduced themselves. And explained the purpose of his visit. "We heard you received a dead body of a tourist woman this morning. We would like to have a look."

"Yes, Sir. But, but...," Nimal struggled. He was not sure whether Samson was still inside or already left. He silently blamed himself for taking a smoking break. Usually, the guy doesn't finish anything quickly. Nimal knew it from experience.

The morgue very rarely receives young female corpses. Samson not only uses them for his requirements. But also arrange a few other loyal friends. For years, Nimal made a handsome income by selling them. He didn't want to expose his illegal business now. Even these are foreigners.

"Why? Isn't it here?" asked Major Alwis.

"No. No... Sir. It is here," Nimal wanted to find a way to delay the entrance. Or turn them away if possible. "Sir..., Director sir said not to allow visitors today."

"Nimal... my friend, look... do we need his permission now?" Major Alwis said with a smile. "He wouldn't learn anything. We need to have a look. That's it. We'll come back with permission later if she is a US citizen. We will treat you well for your assistance," He took a packet of Marlboro from his pant pockets and handed it to the attendant. His eyes sparkled, seeing the unfamiliar name on the colorful box.

Looking around for any eavesdroppers, Nimal quickly pocketed the priced package.

He quickly formulated a plan. While walking towards the closed door, he deliberately misstepped and placed his hand on the door to balance himself. The metal door banged with the impact.

"You, OK?" asked Major Alwis, trying to help the attendant.

"Yes... yes, Sir," Nimal said apologetically, adjusting his shirt. "Sorry, Sir. I've been here since yesterday morning. No one else to work... bit tired."

"I can imagine. It's a hectic week for everyone," Major Alwis replied. Lieutenant closely followed him to the building.

Nimal slightly opened one side of the inner door and peeked inside. Instantly, the stringent smell slapped their faces. The two uniformed men did not stir a bit. But Nimal froze on the spot, seeing what was in the morgue. And what was not there.

His friend was lying on the floor. His white sarong and shirt were in disarray. The metal table at the end of the hall was empty. The dead white woman was nowhere to be seen.

Major Alwis was already on Nimal's heels, keeping one hand on the door.

"Nimal, we won't take long. Let's go inside. Where is it?"

"Sir...," the attendant hesitated. The two soldiers were already inside the gruesome hall. "Sir, it is not here."

"What...? What do you mean it is not here?" Major shared a glance with his partner. Both noticed the body on the floor. One in fresh clothes. And curved like a fetus. All three hurried towards the corpse.

Trembling in fear, Nimal pointed to the table. "It was here when I came last time." Then, turned toward Samson. "He is from a funeral home. He came to pick up a body. What has happened to him?"

Nimal squatted at his friend's body and stared at the shirt pocket. A bundle of money was still there. The two soldiers crouched at the body as well. The medical officer checked the pulse. The face of the dead man was covered in fresh blood. And the front of his white shirt. A pair of opened eyes were looking at the dirty ceiling.

Major Alwis moved one side of the unbuttoned shirt and showed it to his partner. There was an angry red bruise in the middle of the chest. Lieutenant Wadell readily recognized what it was. A female fist. A strong punch on the solar plexus.

Seemingly, a single stab was enough to knock out the young man.

The medical officer looked at his partner. Major Alwis nodded and stood up to leave. For them, it was clear what had happened here. Although difficult to explain.

"Thank you, Nimal," the major pat on his shoulder. "Looks like there's no need for permission anymore." He walked towards the door with his companion.

"Sir... sir...," Nimal struggled to form a question. He couldn't understand any of this.

"Don't worry, she was not dead. We will find her," said Major Alwis. "You might have to tell the director everything you know."

Nimal watched the two uniforms disappear beyond the door. Quickly, he pulled the bundle of cash from Samson's pocket. No one, except for the dead, was watching.

#

Corporal Sandra Showers drove the Humvee along the white, sandy beach full of rubbles. Her task was to pick up four officers from a local temple. She dropped the duo earlier at the monastery devastated by the tsunami. The Marines were helping to clean up and rebuild the place where many devotees died from the waves.

Sandra decided to take the route along the beach for a reason. It was much easier to drive on the sand than on the broken roads. Previously carpeted roads were unidentifiable in some places. Large chunks of the carpet layer had been flushed away by the tides. And some sections were still not cleared of debris. At one place, a crumpled communication tower sat like a massive ball of strings made up of metals. The beach was relatively debris-free. The same waves that made the destruction had flushed most objects on the beach back into the ocean.

Besides, she enjoyed the sea breeze and the beauty of the bright blue horizon. It was hard to believe the same sea acted as a monster a week ago. She drove at a reasonable speed while watching the white waves and endless blue. Suddenly, she noticed a movement in front of her.

"What the fuck?" Sandra cursed to herself while slamming the break. The bulk of the massive truck shuddered in response.

The woman who appeared out of nowhere was standing in front of the vehicle. Merely a foot away from the steaming hood of the Humvee.

"Are you okay?" shouted Sandra, still standing on the brake pedal.

The white woman with blonde hair stared across the windshield. The unusually yellowish eyes did not blink. Her expressionless face didn't give a clue. Sandra had a hard time analyzing the situation. Her initial calculation was that the woman must be a stranded tourist looking for help. The corporal opened the door and stepped outside.

"Are you okay? ...do you need help?" she asked while walking toward the front of the truck. The woman was in a plain white T-shirt and a pair of jeans. But no footwear. No sign of any other possessions.

"What can I do for you? Do you need a ride?" asked Sandra. She genuinely thought the woman was in distress. She placed her hand on the stranger's shoulder as a gesture of friendship.

The marine felt uneasy when the woman continued to stare without a word. Her right hand involuntarily went towards the weapon on her belt. In the next split second, everything changed. First, the woman took the soldier's weapon without much trouble. Sandra was on the ground, bleeding from her mouth and nose.

The woman in uniform stared at her enemy in disbelief. She was a marine with rigorous training and more than five years of experience in the combat field. Sandra could not comprehend what had just happened. The mysterious woman defeated her. Even before she realized it.

The blonde woman bent down and carefully scanned her captive's face. Sandra blankly stared at the yellow irises. But she didn't recognize how the stranger's face transformed into something familiar. The short blonde hair became a long black ponytail. The white skin slowly converted to black. The same color as her own skin. The new facial features of the mystery woman were so familiar to the marine. Suddenly, she realized why. She felt a shock along her spine. It was her own face. She was looking at herself. Like she was in front of a mirror. Except her replica was standing with a weapon aimed at her.

Sandra was defenseless against this mysterious woman who shapeshifted in a few seconds. Suddenly, the marine was stunned by another blow to the head. She did not feel anything when her combat outfit was taken away. The next moment, the Humvee U-turned and started to race toward the city. Corporal Sandra Showers was lying on the beach in her underwear, unconscious.

#

"What the fuck is going on?" General McMaster barked, rushing to the control room. Everyone in the cramped chamber went silent and stood to salute their boss.

"At ease... fill me in."

"Sir, we have a problem," the radio chief said. "The Humvee went to pick up the officers from the temple was missing."

"How the hell has that happened? This is not a combat mission. There were no known threats like that," the general said.

"Sir, it left the camp an hour ago. It's more than enough time to pick up the subjects and return."

"What about GPS records?"

The radio chief directed his boss towards a workstation.

"We checked its path, Sir. It is strange. The Humvee mysteriously U-turned at the beach on its way to the destination. Then it showed up at the landing port half an hour ago. It is still there." The general checked the map on the screen. A red dot showed at the edge of the bay. That was where their shore party landed a few days ago.

"Who the hell ordered it to go there?"

"Sir, there was no communication after it left the camp."

"Call the landing port."

"Sir, we have a problem there. It is dead silent as well." The officer typing hard on his computer said, without changing his rhythm. "Sir, there's another problem. The LCAC waiting at the landing port had gone to the Richards... without any authorization from here."

They had only one hovercraft on standby at the landing port. Without an order from the general himself or the commander of the USS Bonhomme Richards, it shouldn't move from the station.

"What the fuck is going on here," the general said for the second time.

"Sir, the LCAC entered the well-deck ten minutes ago." Another officer informed. His monitor showed a different map. The aircraft carrier and its associate ships were marked on a dark grey background in the middle of the sea.

"Excuse me, Sir. We have an incoming communication from the Richards," the radio chief shouted from his desk. "Sir, Rear Admiral Allen, transferring to station four."

The officer in front of the computer with images of ships picked up the phone. And quickly handed it to General McMaster behind him.

"Gen McMaster, we have a situation here. One of the F35s took off from the deck. Without any authorization," Rear Admiral Allen Davidson said. McMaster listened with an open mouth.

"The pilot was found unconscious in a restroom. Someone has stolen the bird. All communication has been disabled since the takeoff. No radar detections as well." General McMaster shook his head in disbelief. How on earth is it possible to steal a fighter jet from the highly guarded assault ship. But one thing was clear. It is the same person who took the Humvee under his watch.

"Sir, we need to confirm this. But we have a similar situation here," said the general. "One of our Humvees had moved to the landing port without permission. We believe it was taken by force. It could be the same person who entered the mother ship on the stolen LCAC."

While two high-ranking officers were engaged in an embarrassing and animated discussion, several telephones rang in unison.

One call was from the local hospital. They reported a black woman found unconscious on the beach. The locals had brought the girl to the emergency ward. The authorities wanted to confirm whether the woman was a Marine. By the description, the staff members readily identified the woman as the missing Corporal Sandra Showers.

The other call was from a Sergeant stationed at the landing port. The same place the missing Humvee was stationed for half an hour. And no communication was possible until now. The driver of the stolen truck attacked all four soldiers. According to his report, the woman was fast and agile. She had managed to tackle all four guys within seconds. When the Sergeant on guard regained consciousness, the

LCAC was missing from the beach. He requested immediate medical assistance for his colleagues.

#

General Collin McMaster carefully listened to Corporal Sandra Showers, the driver of the stolen Humvee. He understood that there could be something more to this developing situation. No one had ever stolen a fighter jet from the US forces. Maybe some ground vehicles. Mostly when those were abandoned as a defense tactic.

Earlier, the injured marine was transferred from the local hospital to the sick bay of the camp. She was in good health except for a few bruises. The general listened carefully to his soldier. Even though her narration was unbelievable. At first, it didn't make any sense. Losing the Humvee is one thing. But who can believe that someone can transform her shape? And acquire someone else's form? The medical officer confirmed the driver was in good mental health.

The officers who went to inspect the landing port found the four injured soldiers. All but one was still unconscious when the search party arrived at the makeshift camp.

Everything was in order, except for the missing hovercraft. Nothing else was stolen. The only person who could talk was frightened and in shock. Sergeant Roger Williams recounted what had happened. He remembered Corporal Showers speeding into the beach in her Humvee. He observed the same shape-shifting behavior Sandra described. This time from Corporal Showers to Roger Williams. That was after disabling the other three soldiers in a few seconds. The scene was straight out of science fiction.

"We are dealing with something unknown," General McMaster said to his deputy. "Don't think this a local terrorist group. Or a ghost. Whoever is doing this knows everything about us and our work."

They walked to the communication room, bustling with activities. Many were animatedly typing on their keyboards. Others were whispering to their headphone mics. Computer monitors were glowing in many different patterns.

"Contact the CMC," the General said to his radio chief. Within seconds, the line was established, as the commandant was expecting this call at any time.

"Sir, I assume you've already received the reports. Why and what don't we know about this?" General McMaster asked his superior after the introduction.

"Collin, I understand your frustration. But we needed to confirm a few things. Now we have a better picture. This is linked to the submarine that disappeared earlier," the commandant said.

"Sir, what is it? ...If you informed us earlier, we could take some precautions," McMaster said, trying not to show his displeasure.

"Listen... this is a highly classified project. A real secret squirrel," said the commandant. He paused for a moment and explained what had happened. "The navy retrieved an unidentified object, an underwater vessel... two days before the tsunami. This organism, whatever it is, was in the vessel. Its capabilities are unmatched. To secure the alien and avoid its escape, we decided to keep it in the sub."

"Why in the Indian Ocean?"

"That's where the vessel was found. Our intention was to transport it here as it was. But it had a self-destroying mechanism. We lost it before taking it on board a transport ship." The commandant continued.

"Luckily, we could save the sole occupant... and the submarine was in the close vicinity. We transferred the organism to avoid an escape. Your fleet was there to provide security in an emergency."

Oh great. McMaster thought. *Without telling us.*

"Sir, do we know what it is? Is it an alien? Or some device developed by a foreign adversary?"

"We know very little. But... scientists onboard the sub managed to analyze tissue samples. It was not definitely an earthling."

"So, an alien?"

"We believe so."

"How the hell did it escape the sub?"

"That's the mystery here. No communication from it since the tsunami. It could be a malfunction in the nuclear reactors."

If it can damage a nuclear-powered submarine, stealing a Humvee or an F-35 should be a piece of cake, McMaster thought.

"The tsunami shouldn't knock down the sub," said the General.

"Clearly, we underestimated the capabilities of this alien," said the commandant. "The president already met with other counterparts, including China and Russia. They are cooperating with us. This is a global security threat now."

"Sir, how do we tell them? We had this for a week and lost it... This is embarrassing," said McMaster.

"Incident in the sub is off the record. Our official version is it appeared after the tsunami."

"Sir, what are our orders now?" asked McMaster.

"Same. But stay vigilant. All evidence suggests it wanted to escape. There's minimal chance of returning it there," said the commandant and hesitated for a moment. "A Chinese surveillance satellite had a ping on an unknown object in the upper atmosphere, above the Antarctic. It could be the mothership. That's an ideal place to avoid our satellites and other surveillance mechanisms. Be prepared. We might need all of your firepower on short notice."

General McMaster felt uncertain for the first time in his career. In all his combat life, he fought with a known enemy.

But, in this instance, knowledge about the adversary is next to nothing.

#

Dan Chimsky

The Sphere

Dan Chimsky

It was a pleasant evening. The Sun was still a long way from the horizon. A dad and a daughter leisurely walked with their dog on the deserted footpath. Suddenly, the canine changed its behavior.

"Sheba," Sue screamed. "...stop pulling me."

The dog walked swiftly, with her nose fixed to the ground. Sniffing harder in a zigzag pattern. The massive German Shepherd was too strong for the thirteen-year-old girl. Sheba is almost two years old but has grown to her full size. Once she picks up a scent, even Sue's dad can't control the dog.

"Dad... ask her to stop," she shouted while running behind the dog.

Kyle watched this battle between the two loved ones with amusement. On her thirteenth birthday, he advised Sue to train herself in proper dog handling. Not just cuddling. That was only a few weeks ago. So far, she was doing fine, except for occasional incidents like this.

Kyle whistled to the dog to get her attention. Instantaneously, Sheba stopped. But only for a moment to look back. In the next moment, she was on her trail again. Kyle decided that it was time to intervene. He quickened his steps to close the gap with Sue. And took the leash from her hands.

Sheba slowed down a little. But, still, she was hurrying towards her target, with her nose zigzagging on the ground.

"I think she has picked up a scent, probably something unusual," Kyle said.

"Maybe another pile of poo...," she said. "That's what she does all the time."

"Is that so? Why is that?"

"I know... I know... she is gathering information. About other dogs," Sue said excitedly. She knew that her dad was testing her. Sue was fascinated when her dad described dog sniffing behavior a few weeks ago. Then, she learned more by googling the same. Accordingly, dogs can learn many by sniffing the feces and urine of other dogs. Still, she doubted whether dogs could differentiate big dogs from puppies from the smell alone.

"That must be a pile of a big dog. That's why Sheba is so excited," Sue said, following her dad.

They were walking fast on a grassland outside of the city limit. The duo preferred this place because the area is usually devoid of other people or dogs. Sue was still nervous walking Sheba in crowded places.

Sheba quickened her pace. Kyle noticed an opening among the grass blades and dandelions. Something white was in the middle of the green and yellow. Now, closer to her target, Sheba was darting in that direction, pulling Kyle behind her. Less than five meters away from it, Kyle recognized the object. A rabbit... a dead one, to be exact.

Once they reached it, He ordered Sheba to sit. She sat panting and looked at her owner proudly.

"Good girl."

"Yeow...," Sue yelled, covering her mouth. "It's disgusting."

"It's been dead at least for a couple of days, I guess," Kyle said while petting Sheba's head. The carcass was dried up by the hot summer sun. There was no pungent smell or maggots.

"What must have happened to it?" Sue asked.

"Hmm, I don't know. These little ones are very fragile. Even a small impact is enough to kill it. Definitely not a coyote or a dog."

"Why?"

"If it is a predator like Coyote, it should eat the bunny."

"Then, how?"

Suddenly, Sheba stood with her ears erect. And placed her nose on the ground again. The leash had enough slack for her to move away from the carcass. Both father and daughter curiously observed the dog's path. It didn't go too far. Just a couple of meters and stopped. The shepherd looked back invitingly at her master. Sue quickly jumped over tall grass and reached her pet.

"Dad... come quick, look at this." She shouted with excitement. "A ball."

Kyle walked toward them. Indeed, there was a ball. But not any ordinary-looking ball. He crouched next to Sheba to observe the strange object.

It was slightly bigger than a tennis ball. The metallic surface was polished. No dust or scratch marks at all. Something similar to a part of a bearing. Kyle looked back at the dead rabbit and back at the ball.

"Maybe somebody had thrown it here and accidentally hit on Rabbit's head," Sue lamented.

"Hmm... That's possible," Kyle said hesitantly. But he was thinking of the bizarre object. He had never seen anything like that before. To him, it didn't look like an object someone would throw randomly.

"Don't think it was here for long," Kyle said. He pulled a poop bag from his pocket and put it around his hand like a glove.

"Are you going to pick it up?" asked Sue.

"Let's examine what it is."

Kyle picked up the object. As he expected, it felt heavy on his hand. Definitely, more than a baseball. But not as weighty as a rock of the same size.

"It looks amazing," Sue suggested, watching it closely.

"Yes, indeed. It's a perfect globe," Kyle said, surprised by the craftsmanship of the object. It had no markings, no trademark, or anything of that sort.

Kyle placed the ball inside the bag and scanned the surrounding area. The grass was undisturbed, except for the dead rabbit a few feet away. And the footprints made by their boots. There were no signs of any recent human activity.

"Are we taking it home?" Sue asked, with a big smile on her face.

"It's a weird object. Isn't it? I would like to have a better look."

"Dad… could I have it? I can show it to my friends tomorrow."

"We'll see. First, we'll find what it is. I don't think anyone plays with a metal ball like this. It could be a part of some machine. But, hard to guess how it ended up here." He gave the bag to Sue and took the leash. Sheba led the way and stopped for the last time to sniff the carcass.

#

"Sue...," Linda shouted, standing at the base of the staircase. "That's enough of that stupid ball. You have school tomorrow. You better switch off the light and go to bed."

Soon after they arrived home, Sue washed the ball and examined it thoroughly with her dad. All the while, Linda expressed her displeasure for picking up a trash object and bringing it home. Dad and daughter spent more than half an hour. But they couldn't decide what it was. Finally, Kyle lost interest and went to his study. Sue took the sphere to her bed.

"Good night, mom... Good night, Dad," Sue shouted back from her room.

She found her remote for the night lights under her pillows. After switching the LED light strip on, she switched off the ceiling light and crawled under her comforter. She kept her eyes closed, hoping the room would be bright when she opened her eyes again. Finally, she lowered the sheets and peeked.

The room was bright and purple. Not pitch dark anymore. Sue wanted to examine the strange ball one more time. Without getting up, she reached for it on the nightstand. At first glance, the girl realized something had changed. She instantly sat on the bed with the sphere in both hands.

The ball reflected the purple hue of the LED lights. She turned the object in every possible direction to examine the markings on its surface. Something they had not noticed earlier.

"Dad...," she screamed while jumping from her bed, throwing her pillows and sheets in disarray.

She ran along the corridor and towards her dad's office room. Kyle was hurrying towards her when she saw him.

"Are you okay...? What happened?"

Sue barely heard her mom coming out of the kitchen in a hurry.

"Yeah, yeah, yeah...," she replied. "Dad... you need to see this," Sue showed the object. "There are pictures on this." she offered the ball in both hands.

"How come...? There was nothing on it earlier," Kyle said.

"Sue... I told you not to take that to your bed. Throw that stupid ball in the trash can." The father and daughter heard Linda downstairs.

"I don't see anything," Kyle said after turning the object in his hands. "I guess you are too obsessed about it. Now, go to bed. I will keep it in my office. Otherwise, mom will throw it in the garbage."

"No, Dad. I swear I saw it. A line of figures around this, right around the middle," Sue said while taking the object from her dad.

Kyle put his hand in front of her, asking for the object. She reluctantly passed the sphere.

"Dad," she said, lowering her voice. "Maybe it appears in the purple light in my room. I think this light is too bright to see the marks. That's why we don't see it anymore."

"Let's go there. But you are not going to keep this in your room. Okay?" Sue reluctantly nodded her head.

The two entered the room illuminated in purple. Kyle pushed the door behind them.

"See that... Can you see it?" Sue excitedly pointed to the ball.

It took a moment to adjust his eyes to the dim light. Sue was right. Kyle didn't expect this. The purple light in her room changed the object's appearance. It started to glow in purplish blue, reflecting the color in the room. But there was a series of markings along the circumference. Equidistantly placed. Each one is not more than a centimeter. Kyle tried to feel it on his ring finger. But the surface was smooth as chalk.

"Looks like some pictographs," Kyle said.

"Like in pyramids?"

"Don't think these are the same. Not like letters of any common language we know. But who knows? There are thousands of languages in the world."

"But dad... why does anyone want to drop it here in Canada?"

"You know what...? We should report this. And give it to... probably to the museum."

"Dad... why can't we keep it?"

"No... whatever it is, you are not going to keep it in this house," Linda said, leaning on the door frame. The duo hadn't realized she was silently watching all this time.

"Okay, we'll see it tomorrow. Now, you go to bed. I will keep it in my office room," said Kyle. Sue reluctantly climbed into her bed.

#

"Dad...," Kyle heard a scream from his office room downstairs. He was in his bedroom, getting ready to go to work.

"Dad... come here quick. You should see this," Sue shouted again.

Suddenly, Kyle remembered the object they had retrieved the previous night. After Sue went to bed, he examined the sphere with various light configurations in his study. There were twelve tiny markings on the metal surface. And appeared under dim light. Probably something to do with the wavelength of the spectrum, he concluded. Countless searches to find similar figures on the internet came fruitless. Tired of working so late into the night, he decided this could be the work of a local artist. But lost somehow in the prairies.

"Dad... are you coming?" Sue called him again. "Now, there are two."

"What?" Kyle ran towards his office room while buttoning his shirt.

"See this... there are two of them here." Sue showed her palms. Balancing on her hands, two identical spheres. Those were the same as the one they picked last night. But smaller. About two-thirds of the original object.

"But... but, how?" Kyle was speechless. "How is it even possible? I kept it here last night." He got one from Sue's hand. It was as smooth as the one they picked. No markings were visible. His eyes switched between his and his daughter's hands.

"You didn't do that, right?" Sue asked, frowning at him. Kyle understood her suspicions.

"No, dear, how do I do that? Those are perfect shapes. I don't think I can create such a thing."

"Kyle, don't you go to work today?" They heard Linda in the kitchen. "Sue, you are already late for school."

Before going to school, she thought to check the strange object. Sue sneaked into her dad's office room to have a look. In fact, she wanted to show the sphere to her friends. But she forgot all those when she noticed what had happened. Instead of one, now there are two.

"You go now. I will take care of this. Otherwise, you know mom will throw this in the garbage bin."

Seeing the mysterious duplication of the object, Kyle could not decide what to do next. He was puzzled more than his daughter. Finally, he decided to lock the two items in his drawer and find a solution later. He turned the objects around and examined them one last time before leaving the study.

"You are spoiling that kid," Linda said. Kyle was having his breakfast in the kitchen.

"Oh... don't worry, it's a silly game." Kyle tried to smile. But he was still wondering what was going on. They found it at an unusual place. Then, they found mysterious markings. And the sphere reproduced itself during the night like a living organism.

"Don't bring such rubbish into the house. Who knows what those things come with."

"Honey, I'll be late today. Have a meeting in the afternoon. That might drag for hours." Kyle quickly changed the subject. Under the table, he ran his fingers over the pant pockets. The keys to his drawers were with him. Kyle was uncertain why he wanted to hide the new information from his wife.

\#

Sue impatiently ran home after school. She patted Sheba's head and dashed upstairs in a hurry. Threw her bag onto the bed. When she turned back to go downstairs, she noticed it. She couldn't believe her eyes. The object she was longing to play with was in front of her. One of the two miniature spheres was on her desk beside her computer.

"Thx, Dad. ILY," Sue texted.

She forgot all her mom's instructions on what to do after returning from school. Instead, she quickly jumped to the seat in front of her table. And picked the object.

"Where is your brother? Is he in Dad's room? He must be lonely there." Sue talked to the ball in her hand. At the time, Sheba pushed the door and entered the room.

"Hey, Sheba, look at this. You found it. Didn't you?"

The dog sniffed the ball once. Uninterested, she walked out of the room.

"What are you? A magic ball from the pyramids of Egypt? ...Let's find out." She talked to the little sphere, typing her password one-handed. When the screen lit, she placed the ball on the tabletop.

For a moment, Sue thought she had heard something. She had a long look at the sphere beside the keyboard.

Sue took the ball and kept it pressed to her left ear. Other than the coldness of metal on her skin, there was no sound.

"Silly girl... how does a metal ball talk to you? It is not an animal." Sue murmured to herself and placed the object back on the table.

"Come on, Google... hurry up," she said, shaking her head with frustration. The loading icon in the middle reluctantly moved in circles.

"Let's do a little search if we can find anything about you." She talked to the sphere again while waiting.

Sue started to type, then deleted and punched again. She was not sure what to search for.

"No, no... not that... Let's say metal spheres found in pyramids." She hit the enter key.

Nothing interesting. Sue changed the search page to images. It was full of stone objects. Some were of massive sizes, larger than humans. Apparently, those are from everywhere in the world. But most are from South and Central America. Fascinated by these strange artifacts, she almost forgot her initial intention. She skimmed through several articles.

Suddenly, the sphere on her table rolled. Scared, Sue almost jumped out of her seat. She involuntarily took her hand from the mouse. And pushed her legs to move away from the table. The chair rolled back and stopped at her bed. Not far enough. Sue stared at the ball. The object had stopped an inch away from the mouse. She couldn't believe what had just happened.

How does it move on its own?

In the corner of her eye, she saw a photo of a stone orb on her screen. The caption said, Ancient Aliens. She quickly sat on the chair with her legs curled. Reluctantly, she dragged her body towards the table again. And slowly moved the mouse away from the object and clicked on the photo.

"Are you an alien? Can you hear me?" She asked the ball, lowering her voice. It didn't move.

"Is it observing me? or what I'm doing? Did it move to see what's on the monitor?"

The joy of having the object for herself to play with vanished. The fear started to creep in. Sue looked around to see whether Sheba was around. But the dog was nowhere to be seen. The thought of someone watching her sent a chill along her back. Suddenly, she felt lonely and afraid. Both mom and dad are at work. She didn't want to stay alone with the ball anymore.

Sue slowly moved her chair without taking her eyes off the metal object. When she had enough space between the table and chair, she jumped. And ran towards the door without looking back. Within seconds, she was outside the house with Sheba. Sue didn't see where the sphere settled next.

#

Kyle parked the SUV on the driveway. When he opened the front door, he heard laughter and growling in the backyard. From the window, he saw Sue throwing a ball at Sheba.

Kyle went straight to the office room. Placed the bunch of folders on the table. Suddenly, he felt something was not right. He looked around the room. And back at the table. Everything was in order. Except for one.

Someone had opened the drawer on his desk. The quick scan suggested nothing was missing. Then, he remembered about the sphere mysteriously replicated overnight. Both objects were not there. He remembered how he locked them in the drawer.

When he was about to scream his daughter's name, he noticed another unusual. The low hum of his desktop computer he rarely uses. The screen was black. But the machine was running in the background.

Kyle bent down and moved the mouse. The screen illuminated instantly. His minimalist desktop appeared. No programs were in use. Kyle blankly stared at the monitor. He was sure he didn't boot the machine in several days. The previous night, he worked on his laptop. Which was still in his bag hanging on his shoulder. No one else in the family uses his computer or his office room.

Confused, he placed his bag on the floor and pulled his car keys from his pockets. Suddenly, he saw the keys to the drawers. He thought Sue somehow managed to open the drawer and take the objects to play with. But it is very unusual for her daughter to do such a thing. Then he remembered the text message from her. At the time, he didn't pay attention as he was in a meeting. He pulled out the phone. He couldn't think of anything special he did to thank at the time.

Kyle thoroughly searched the drawers and the tabletop. Then he scanned the room. He couldn't see the strange spheres anywhere within the walls.

When he came downstairs, Sue was back inside with the dog. Sheba came, rushing towards him, wagging her tail.

"Where's mom?"

"Mom went shopping," she said. "Dad... are aliens real?" She sat comfortably on the couch, expecting a long discussion. That's the usual girl, thought Kyle.

"There is no evidence. I mean... no concrete evidence," Kyle said while looking for a mug. He was happy to see the hot coffee pot on the machine. "But there are sightings all over the world. Why do you ask?" He suppressed his urge to inquire about the drawer and missing spheres.

"Dad... something strange happened this afternoon," said Sue. Kyle sat on the loveseat opposite her with his coffee.

Sue explained what had happened in the afternoon. About her web search and how the sphere moved on her table. And her thoughts about aliens. Kyle silently listened with little to no encouragement. He wanted to inquire how she opened the drawer. He waited until she finished her story.

"Dad, could that be an alien object?" Sue asked. "I felt like it was observing me. I heard a little chime once... like it was trying to talk to me."

Kyle placed his mug on the coffee table. "It is possible someone created that object to spy on others. That's very common these days." Kyle said, thinking about other possibilities.

"Sue, I have a question. How did you open my drawer? Where is the other one now?" Kyle asked finally.

"What drawer?" She asked, straightening up on the couch. Sheba walked towards her. Sue placed one hand on the dog's back.

Kyle didn't want to scold his daughter. He described what he saw in his office room.

"No, Dad... I didn't go there. I thought you kept one in my room this morning after I left for school. I saw it when I came home. Didn't you receive my text?" Sue asked.

"Let's go and see your room," Kyle said. Apparently, Sue had not gone to her room after the incident.

"You go first," Sue said, getting off the couch.

When they arrived in her bedroom, it was dark. Kyle switched on the ceiling light.

The desktop computer had gone to sleep. No hum. Nothing unusual. But the object was not on the table. Not anywhere to be seen.

"Where is it?" asked Kyle.

"It was here when I ran out of the room. I'm pretty sure," Sue pointed towards the mouse. Both scanned the room to see whether it was somewhere else. Kyle moved her pillows on the bed. Sue searched her school bag and closet. No sign of the mysterious sphere.

In the next few minutes, the two frantically searched all possible places in Sue's bedroom. And also Kyle's office room. In the end, they decided to call off the effort. As it mysteriously doubled the previous night, those were gone without a trace.

Frustrated, the father and daughter settled on the couch. The conversation between the two dragged on about ancient technologies. Kyle was still in his office attire. He finished his coffee and stood from his seat.

Sheba got up from her sleep and walked towards the front door. In a moment, Linda came with multiple bags.

"Hello, mom," Sue greeted her mother.

"You are early... I thought you would be late today," Linda said to Kyle.

"Yes, the meeting finished a little earlier. We lost internet for a couple of hours." Kyle kissed her cheek and helped her to bring groceries to the kitchen.

"Mom... did you throw our spheres?" Sue asked, stroking Sheba's head.

"Don't ask me. Why? ...did you lose it?" Linda asked while opening the fridge. Kyle noticed a faint smile on her face. She seems to be happy to hear that objects are missing.

"You took it from Dad's drawer. Didn't you?"

"It's good you lost it. Now, come and help me here." Linda demanded the girl. Kyle shrugged and went to his office. He knew that any discussion with his wife had to be later.

#

Kyle stayed staring at the screen in disbelief. The breaking news was all over the news sites. It had begun several hours ago. But somehow, he missed the news.

Several pilots of the US Air Force had reported an unidentified flying object. For a long time, the government did not publicly discuss UFO sightings. But things have changed. The authorities don't hide these observations anymore. So, the news was out. Fighter jets were on a practice mission in an undisclosed area when the UFOs were observed. But, before the Pentagon released a statement, several others had reported the incident on social media.

Unlike countless previous sightings of UFOs, this was photographed and live-streamed by some observers. The most unusual of the reports was the direction of the UFO's flight. According to a fighter jet pilot who videoed the UFO, it was moving fast against gravity. Towards the upper atmosphere and beyond. The sighting was first reported at around 5 p.m. Pacific time. As per the news, NASA officials are conducting further investigations.

CNN reported a similar activity two days ago, citing a lesser-known website dedicated to UFO sightings. That was in the Indian Ocean south of Maldives. The live broadcast repeatedly brought back the past footage of interviews. Some people in several fishing vessels had seen five bright red lights falling from the sky. Based on those eyewitness accounts, five objects were moving fast toward the earth. On a straight line, keeping equal distance between them. Close to the water's surface, the objects radiated in different directions. Within a few seconds, all were out of sight on the horizon. No one thought of those as space crafts or drones. Because those were too fast and too small to be any man-made machine.

Could the sphere we collected be one of those flying objects? Kyle couldn't stop thinking about it.

It was a masterpiece of metallurgy. A perfect globe. And the pictographs were unique. Kyle's internet searches to find any resemblance came empty. Mysterious duplication overnight was unexplainable. It seems to have a self-replication mechanism. He had no other explanation. Then, the two identical objects escaped from the locked drawer. He was sure Linda didn't do that. Sue's account of how the sphere moved on her table added further suspicions. She was searching the internet about aliens at the time. Could there be a link?

Suddenly, he went rigid. A thought flashed in his mind. Were those spheres spying on humans? He started to type on his laptop, praying this shouldn't be the case.

He spent the next half hour jumping from one page to the next without reading the complete article. But skimming through the headlines. And the first paragraph was enough to connect the dots.

All three tech giants, who own the world's largest cloud storage units, reported a slowdown since midnight yesterday. And it was a considerable malfunction that lasted more than fifteen hours. Kyle realized what had happened in the office. No one could log into company databases. The IT guys were struggling to find a solution without any success.

Media reported that it had been resolved on its own an hour ago. The engineers are still working on finding the possible causes of this unusual activity. Something never happened in the history of cloud computing. The Department of Defence declared that there's no foreign adversary involved in it. The breakdown occurred everywhere in the world, including in China and Russia.

Meanwhile, A Ph.D. student at MIT tweeted that someone was downloading everything on the internet. Since then, the post got the attention of millions of subscribers, shattering all previous retweeting records.

"Not by someone," Kyle murmured to himself. "They now know everything about us, our history, and what we know about the universe. But we know nothing about them."

The Prediction

Dan Chimsky

It was the most memorable Friday in all his life. It was the day that changed his dreams forever. The memory of the incident haunted him for the last twenty-five years. What happened that day was the only reason he was facing three armed aliens now. Scenes were unfolding as accurately as he foresaw on that fateful day.

Edmond MacArthur, the mayor of the city, did not know whom he was dealing with. He blankly stared at the stocky man in front of him. And two others on his flanks. All in black uniforms. And armed. The distant memories started to flood his mind.

That was a quarter century ago. The last day of the work week started like any other usual morning. Eddie rode his bike to work. He was determined to enjoy the last few sunny mornings of the fall. But he forgot one thing. An obvious one. That is, it was a Friday. The day, all his friends gather at the downtown nightclub *The Owls*. That's where all his journalist colleagues, young and old, male and female, take refuge on Friday nights. Drown their grievances of the week. Find ideas to write for the next week. Most of all, get drunk. The bicycle is not the best mode of transport for such a day.

Eddie was the youngest member of the club. Graduated only a few months prior. And joined the newspaper as an intern. He was one of the few singles in the group and had the luxury of meeting every week. Understandably, he was one of the last to leave the club, well after midnight.

As on many other Friday nights, Eddie was drunk to his uppermost limit on that fateful day. He barely managed to ride his bike along the deserted streets of the old city. An hour after midnight, he crossed the bridge that marks the city limit.

Eddie had to cross the cemetery before reaching the trailer park where he lived. The gravel road bisects the century-old graveyard into two perfect halves. Two long rectangles covered with ancient cottonwoods. That's where things went wrong. Or got interesting, as he thought for the last twenty-five years.

As a young graduate, Eddie thought he could change the world. He refused to work for his family business. Instead, joined a lesser-known regional newspaper. He rented a mobile home at the trailer park, ignoring his parents' objections. They lived five hundred miles away in a multi-million-dollar mansion. He was their only son and heir to a business empire.

The couple dismissed his idea of becoming an award-winning journalist. But, allowed, for the time being, assuming he would quickly learn a life lesson. Being rebellious, Eddie thought to get some real-time experience by living with a different section of society. It was a dream life for a rich kid of an elite family. Hookers, drug dealers, smugglers, and old pensioners were his neighbors at the time.

All his dreams changed on that Friday night. Eddie rode his bicycle to the trailer park and community he loved. The streetlights ended at the bridge. Eddie had no option other than riding along the darkened gravel road. He was mad at himself. It's not because he was spooked by the cemetery. But riding the bike when he was drunk was a nightmare. He was in a condition where even walking was drudgery.

Although he was never superstitious, Eddie felt a chill. Suddenly, he saw something crossing the road, just a dark shape. Like any other drunken man, he was slow to respond. Before realized what it was, he was hit. Instantaneously, Eddie was on the ground with dirt on his face. He tasted blood on his tongue. But didn't feel any other pain.

"Are you okay?" Someone asked. Eddie tried to focus on the person in front of him. Both alcohol and the impact of the accident were in the works. He was not sure whether it was just after he fell or sometime later. He lost the sense of time.

"Yea..ah... I'm Okay... I think," said Eddie.

The guy did not offer to help. He was standing there. Silent as a statue. At the time, Eddie was uncertain whether that was a man or a woman. He barely made the dark human shape.

Eddie had heard and read countless ghost stories. But he never believed those. And never encountered anything mysterious. It was the same road he traveled every day.

On the other hand, it's highly probable someone in the trailer park loiters into this stretch. Even in the early hours of the day. The cemetery was like a playground for the residents. No one cared about the dead.

"What has happened?" The dark figure asked. The voice boomed in the silent forest. Definitely a Man.

"Something crossed the road... maybe a coyote. I guess I hit the poor animal." Eddie struggled to stand up. After a few minutes of fighting with the bike, he managed to control it on the wheels. And he decided to walk the rest instead of riding it.

"Where are you going? To the trailer park?" asked Eddie.

"To the future," said the stranger.

"What the fu...," Eddie murmured himself and said again. "That's interesting."

The stranger didn't say anything. Eddie made another unsuccessful attempt to see the guy's face. But it was too dark to see any detail.

He must be high, thought Eddie. "Okay, Let's go then... To the future," Eddie said the last part louder. Then, started to push his bike toward the trailer park. The dark figure walked beside him.

The gravel road was unlit, the same as any other night. Massive cottonwood trees along the road covered much of the sky, creating a dark tunnel. And it prohibits any light from the moon. But there was a glimmer of light in the distance. The trailer park at the end of the passage.

"Wait... are you from the future?" asked Eddie, hoping to continue the conversation. Having someone to talk to at that time of the night was something rare.

"Maybe... maybe not," the stranger said. "Nevertheless, I can take you there."

Dumbfounded by the answer, Eddie stopped and stared at the man beside him.

"To which year?" asked the stranger without looking at Eddie.

"Let me think...," Eddie decided to play along. "Okay, I'm twenty-five now. Let's go and see me when I'm fifty. Twenty-five years from now," said Eddie, smiling to himself. He was glad he found a companion to walk with him. Even though it was crazy to talk about time traveling with a stranger in a cemetery.

"There's so much to see in the future. Why do you want to see yourself?"

For the first time, Eddie noticed the uncharacteristically low pitch of his companion. He tried to match the voice with that of people he knew. Residents of the trailer park. But He couldn't.

"I don't think the world would change that much in twenty-five years. But I will be old. Isn't it?" asked Eddie, pushing his bike again. "By the way, what do you do there in the future? Why did you come back?"

"That's not important."

"Aha, you are… You are from the future," said Eddie. The stranger didn't say anything.

Since there was no response, Eddie thought the conversation was over. Both walked silently for another minute or two.

"Okay, I will take you there… to see your future. You can spend two days there. Only two days," the stranger said. Eddie was happy to hear from his odd companion again.

"I accept your offer, my lord," said Eddie playfully. "Would there be booze? Or some weeds?"

"There are. But you are not allowed." He turned towards Eddie. "I warn you. If you make a mistake, you lose twenty-five years of your life."

"What does that mean? I can't come back if I drink or smoke there?" Eddie asked, trying to see the stranger's face.

Eddie was not sure whether it was alcohol or something else. He started to feel weird. He attempted to remind himself what had happened. His bike hit something. Then, the stranger appeared from nowhere like a ghost. And offered to take him to the future with him. Now, the guy has some conditions.

"Oww... Wait, wait. Where are you taking me?"

"To where you asked..., to the future."

"Who are you? What is your name?" Eddie asked hesitantly. He didn't want to confront this man in an isolated place. The guy was clearly a foot taller. And heavily built by the look of the shape in the dark.

"Does it matter?" The man said in his usual manner and started to walk again. Eddie followed in silence.

The lights at the end of the road began to glow brighter. The strobes penetrated through the dense, tall vegetation in the cemetery.

That's unusual, thought Eddie. Not the faint old lights of the trailer park. He wondered whether the shabby mobile homes were on fire. But the illuminations were constant and more whitish than a fire. Almost like daylight. Coming from above, not the direction of the trailer park. And there was no smell of burning wood smoke.

Eddie silently studied the stranger. Although the gravel path was still dark, there was enough light to see some shades and shapes. The stranger had a deathly white face and long white hair. At least, that's what Eddie saw at the time. The man was not disturbed by Eddie's inspection. Or seeing the strange brightness in the distance.

Suddenly, he turned towards Eddie and said, "You are almost there."

"What is this game? You don't live in the trailer park. I haven't seen you visiting there either."

"No."

"Then... what is this? Who are you?" Eddie almost screamed. By that time, he knew it was not alcohol. He was sure that he was in good consciousness. Not drunk anymore.

"I'm keeping a promise."

"What promise?" asked Eddie.

"Don't you remember? You requested to go and see your future. I'm taking you there. That's all." The man smiled. They were almost at the end of the cemetery, where the trees started to thin.

Eddie started to protest, then suddenly saw the light source. He lost his grip on the bike he was pushing. It fell on the ground. Eddie rushed towards the edge of the tree line.

Within seconds, he was in the clearance. He couldn't believe what he was looking at.

"What the fuck is that?"

An enormous globe was hanging low in the sky. It looked so close. Eddie thought he could touch it if he jumped a little higher.

He didn't see the other strange things for a while because he was focused on the object. It was an exact replica of the moon. Except, it is much closer.

His strange companion caught up with him.

"It's the night light... Nuclear powered."

Eddie tried to see the real one. But the brightness obscured any other object in the sky. No moon, no stars. Not even the sky. He felt a chill along his spine. Eddie slowly turned towards the man beside him.

"Are... we...," Eddie struggled, "...are we in the future?"

The man nodded with a faint smile. Then, Eddie noticed the unusual features of his companion, now illuminated by the artificial moonlight. He was in a pair of pants that looked like metallic suits in old Star Trek movies. The jacket was of the same material but a slightly different color shade. More purplish than the pants. The most unusual was the scar across his face. From left eye to chin, there was a dark, thin mark of an old wound. The long white hair that flowed over his shoulders reminded the Witcher. The pale iris and hair gave him a ghostly look. Eddie noticed an earpiece on his left ear.

"Aren't we? Look around." The man took his backpack and started to open it when Eddie hesitantly turned around.

"What the hell," Eddie struggled again to find words. "What has happened to the trailer park? What is this place?" He had so many questions. None of the things he saw around made any sense. The trailer park was gone. Instead, there was a massive, square-shaped building with metal sidings.

In every direction, except where they came, there were square shapes. All metallic. And even the road. Nice and clean. No dirt or gravel. Everything was well illuminated by the low-hanging moon.

"Welcome to the future," the man said, standing behind him. Eddie could not believe what he was hearing. Speechless, his eyes went back to the moon.

"That's your night light. You don't need streetlights. By the way... I'm Devin. And you might need this." He handed over a transparent face mask. And took one for himself from the backpack.

"I'm Eddie... thanks. But why this?" Eddie took the facemask reluctantly. It felt soft in his hands.

"The air may not be good to breathe. And it's the law. Everyone should wear a mask when going outside. Remember, we are in twenty-five years' future," Devin said. "We need to find some clothes for you too."

"Why? What's wrong with these?"

"You look ancient here. No one dresses like that anymore. Someone could complain to the cops."

"Why should someone call the police for wearing jeans and t-shirts?"

"Man... this is a different time. People are suspicious of everyone. Especially when they see someone in ancient clothes like yours," said Devin and started to walk along the metallic sidewalk. Eddie looked back at the cemetery. He couldn't see anything other than the shades of trees. He was not sure whether the old cemetery was still there. Without questioning, Eddie quickly followed his strange partner.

"Where are the people? I don't see anyone."

"It is past midnight. No one walks randomly in the streets at this time." Devin looked around. "... and at this era. But eyes may be upon us," he added.

"Why?"

"Listen... Things have changed. Twenty-five years is a long time." Devin turned to a narrow road, like a back alley. Eddie closely followed him, fearing he might get lost. They walked several blocks and stopped at the door of one of the tall buildings. It was just a rectangle marked on the metallic wall. No door handle or a door jamb.

Devin tapped on his gadget that resembled a wristwatch. He played with the screen for a few seconds. Then, they heard a soft mechanical sound inside the wall. And the marked rectangle started to slide to one side.

"Is that the key? Do you work here? Or is this your house?"

"No, No, and No," said Devin. "I know how to get around. First, we'll find some clothes for you. This is a store. No one is there at this time."

"Are we stealing?"

"Do you want to wait until opening hours? And pay for your goodies?"

"Don't they have security cameras?"

"Those are things of the past. This is the future. These doors are supposed to be highly secured. But I have my own ways. Don't worry. We would not get caught."

After walking through several hallways, they entered a large hall with apparel. It was similar to fashion stores Eddie was familiar with. Except there were no cashiers.

They picked some clothes that fit Eddie. All in some form of metallic hues. Eddie felt weird in that futuristic dress. To be safe, he packed his old ones into the backpack. Once changed, they walked towards the elevator.

#

Eddie and Devin spent the day exploring the city. In fact, they visited the places carefully selected by Devin. Almost all of them were popular tourist attractions, which were not many and all man-made structures. There were a few structures from the past. Otherwise, it was unlike any city Eddie was familiar with in his real life. It was an expansive metropolitan without an end in sight. In every direction they traveled, buildings of similar shapes and sizes lined up along the metallic road.

They traveled around the city like any other two locals. They received occasional staring from locals. Luckily, no one questioned them.

Eddie started to get bored. Everything he saw was as predicted a long ago.

There were no vehicles run on fossil fuel. All cars were electric and ran with magnetic levitation. All roads were facilitated with maglev technology. But that was ancient. People have been using it for many decades for trains.

Air was polluted to intolerable levels in some parts of the country. Blame the previous generations for not making changes at the right time. There was no smog in the city. But warnings of harmful suspended chemical particles were shown on screens. So, citizens wore masks all the time, except for when they were inside the buildings.

People carried various types of gadgets, from eyeglasses to wristbands. Those had many different functions, like Devin's wristwatch. People are lazy, thought Eddie. Wearable technology gained popularity when Eddie was an undergrad.

No doubt technology has developed during the last three decades.

For the whole time they were exploring the city, Eddie couldn't see a single tree or an animal. Nature was not a part of city life in this era. That was predicted back then as well. Eddie wanted to go outside the metropolis and see the situation there. But he suppressed that urge as he had only a limited time. He had better things to do.

#

"When are we going to see me?" Eddie asked.

Devin was still in his bed, fumbling with a tablet. He silently continued his work on the screen. Eddie looked around the hotel room. It was barely enough for two beds. No tables or other furniture. He looked at his partner again. Only one day of his visit was left. He wondered whether Devin had forgotten his promise. He was fully engrossed in something as there was no one around.

"Later today," said Devin without taking his eyes off the screen.

It was a few hours later, and the issue came again. They were having their lunch at a small street-side restaurant. A fast-food place with a name Eddie did not recognize. There were only three other people, including the server. None of them paid attention to the duo.

"Do you really want to see your old self?" asked Devin, almost like whispering.

"Isn't that the reason we came here? You are the one who promised it."

"What if you don't like it?"

"What do you mean? Do you already know anything about my future?" asked Eddie. He quickly lowered his voice, looking at others in the restaurant. "What has happened to me? Tell me."

"Nothing. I just asked. What could happen in twenty-five years?" Devin said in his usual expressionless tone. And started to munch on his sandwich.

Eddie watched a slow-moving pod through the window. A car on the maglev strip on the road. The street was not busy except for a few occasional pods. Looked like there was no office rush hour.

Devin was right. What could happen to a man in twenty-five years, thought Eddie. But he didn't like the way Devin asked it. Even though they had spent more than a day together, Eddie knew nothing about his companion.

"Devin... I still don't know who you are. Don't know whether even this is real. Two nights ago, I stumbled upon you when I was drunk. Now, here I am, somewhere I don't know." Eddie released his frustration.

"Take it easy, man." Devin finished his coffee. "Let's go where you want to go. I know how to find you."

Eddie was more confused. How does he know where to find one person in a big city like this. Unless he knows something more. Eddie decided to go with the tide, as he's been doing so far. He drained the cup and picked up his backpack.

Once they came to the road, Devin ordered a pod. He just had to punch some numbers on the screen of his wrist gadget. Two minutes later, an empty pod for two stopped in front of them.

"You know where to find me, right?" asked Eddie, once settled on the seats. Devin nodded and signaled to fasten the seat belts. Once they were secured, the pod started to move with a soft *hum*.

"How do you know? Why don't you tell me? What is going to happen?"

"You are impatient. You can see for yourself in a few minutes," Devin said, scanning the surroundings. "Better not to talk those here. There are eyes and ears upon us," he whispered, signaling to the ceiling.

They silently watched passing pods on the otherwise empty streets. There were no people on the sidewalks. After around fifteen minutes of traveling across the city, the vehicle stopped. The duo stepped down to the sidewalk.

"Is this where we go?" asked Eddie. The building in front of them was no different from any other in the city. Of the same size and shape, with the same metal sidings. None of the buildings had name boards or numbers.

"This is a tricky situation. We are not authorized to enter this building at this time. We'll go from the service entrance. Once inside, no one will check us. Stay closer to me. Okay?" Devin started to walk around the building. Eddie reluctantly followed him, wondering what to expect. What is 50-year-old Eddie doing in this building?

"Is this where I work? What is this place?" asked Eddie.

"The city hall," said Devin.

"I'm not a journalist anymore?"

Devin didn't answer. Instead, He started to fumble with his wrist gadget. He used the same trick as he did to enter the clothing store.

Once inside, Devin signaled his partner to be silent. They casually walked towards the main entrance through a maze of hallways. The whole building was deserted. The two didn't see anyone in the office rooms they passed.

"What's going on? Why there's no one in the building?" asked Eddie.

"Seems like we have a problem here," whispered Devin, signaling again to be quiet.

Suddenly, Devin stopped and stepped back. Eddie also saw the four people in the front lobby. At first glance, Eddie knew they were different.

Different from all the other humans they saw for the last two days. All four were shorter and stocky. But pale skinned as

Devin, lighter than any other Eddie knew or seen. All were in black uniforms and carried weapons. Something similar to the automatic machine guns of his era. But smaller. It was not hard to deduce these were in a combat mission.

Devin slowly turned around, grabbed Eddie's arm, and started to walk back the same way they came. The four guards were focused on the front entrance. Therefore, didn't see the two intruders behind them. Eddie led the way through a different set of hallways. But more carefully than the initial entry. Frequently, he consulted the map on his wrist. They didn't see anyone until they turned toward the atrium.

The atrium was a massive space with balconies from five upper stories. Many hallways cascaded to the open space on the ground level. Suddenly, Devin stopped again. And placed his arm to stop Eddie. Immediately, both saw what was ahead of them.

In the atrium, people were on their knees. Silently staring at the marble floor. The few faces the two could see looked frightened and helpless.

The two black uniforms at the end of the hallway blocked their view. Devin silently backtracked, pushing his partner. Eddie's shoes squeaked on the floor for a moment.

"Stoep...," Eddie heard the command in a thick accent. "Doo..n't Moove."

Devin didn't listen. He grabbed Eddie's arm. And started to run. They heard the heavy footsteps behind them. At least two stocky guys. Eddie prayed to God while running. Probably for the first time in his life after middle school. To save him from the bullets of those mercenaries.

After two turns, Devin stopped at a narrow door. And opened it. Quickly pulled Eddie through it. And closed it behind without any noise. They were in a small room. In less than a minute, they heard runners in the hallway. This time, not two. A group. Eddie and Devin listened to the fading footsteps in the distance.

\#

"What the fuck is going on?" Eddie asked, trying to control his rage. He was mad at Devin. But more at himself.

Devin placed the index finger on his lips. "It is a full-blown war. Those have taken people as hostages."

"What war? There was nothing outside."

"It has just begun," Devin whispered, looking around. They were in a mechanical room. Metal tubes and wires were attached to side walls. Devin glanced at the wide opening in the ceiling, where all the cables exited. "We need to move. If we were caught, that would be the end. No going back."

Eddie grabbed Devin's collar. And pulled towards himself. Eddie had to look up, as the guy was at least a foot taller.

"Where the hell are we in? Tell me... what is ..." Suddenly, they heard footsteps in the hallway again. "...going on?" Eddie finished lowering his voice.

Devin didn't speak. But calmly placed his hands on Eddie's clenched fists. He loosened the grip.

Outside, the sounds of the approaching boots got louder. This time, both heard a verbal exchange across the metallic wall. Eddie couldn't understand a word. A different language, something he had never heard.

"They are looking for us," Devin said when the chatter in the hallway faded.

"Who are they?"

Devin didn't answer. Instead, he looked up at the opening in the ceiling. "Let's go through that. We need to find a way out."

"Who are they?" Eddie tried to pull from Devin's shoulder, who was already turning away.

"Does it matter? They are going to kill those people anyway. And both of us, if they found."

"What the fuck? Why are they going to kill people?"

"Don't you have common sense? Do people come with their weapons to party? It's a war. If you want, stay here. And lose half of your life. Do you want to go back to your time or die here?"

It took a few seconds to click. Eddie couldn't believe what he had just heard.

"Does it mean I die today?" Eddie asked, slowly releasing Devin's collar.

"We both die here if we stay arguing forever." Devin started to look around. Then he pushed Eddie away and stepped towards the steel cabinet in the back of the room. Among various tools and gadgets, Devin pulled a folding ladder. He placed it directly under the opening in the ceiling. Eddie realized what his partner was going to do.

"Obviously, we can't walk through the doors. Let's try to find a way out. Those service shafts are not wide or tall enough. We'll have to crawl. Make sure not to make any noise." Devin started to climb toward the ceiling.

Fully extended, the step ladder was not tall enough for Devin to comfortably get into the crawl space. He hung on his hands and lifted his body when Eddie pushed from below. Once inside, Devin helped Eddie to climb. The passageway was barely two feet wide. And the same height. It ran parallel to the hallway down. Metal tubes were fastened to one side wall.

Devin tapped on his wrist gadget. Its glow barely illuminated the cavern. That was enough to see a few feet in front of them. Then, he started to crawl like an infantryman. Silent as a caterpillar.

Eddie followed him, trying hard not to make any noise. His mind was racing in all directions. For a moment, he thought it was a dream. He prayed it would be the case. But, for now, decided to obey his companion. He didn't want to die here, in an unknown place and time.

Eddie watched how easily his partner crawled inside the narrow space without a commotion. Clearly, he was well-experienced in such situations. Still, it was a slow process. Eddie had no idea where they were inside the building. But he saw Devin consult his gadget frequently. He must have a blueprint of the building, thought Eddie.

The two crawled for around twenty minutes, which felt like a half-day for Eddie. Limited space and the necessity of silence made them extremely slow. They had to stop on several occasions whenever they heard sounds below.

The search efforts by the guards had intensified. Now, more guards were walking and running in hallways, frantically scouring for the two men they couldn't shoot earlier. The guards had captured all the employees of the building. And registered visitors. But searching for two unauthorized guests, who they hadn't expected. Devin translated the conversations they heard below for his partner.

Devin stopped at one place where the service passageway had branched. The side tunnel was narrower and much shorter in height. He signaled their next move to Eddie.

"We need to be extra cautious. We are passing a roomful of aliens," Devin whispered.

"Aliens?" He momentarily forgot where he was.

"Shh...," Devin suggested to be silent and started to crawl again. Eddie Followed with much hesitation.

In less than two minutes, they stopped hearing the conversation below. This time, Eddie was sure, the so-called aliens were interrogating someone. The thick accent was unmistakably foreign.

Devin took off his wrist gadget and pulled a thin wire from it. Eddie couldn't see what he was doing. In a minute, the sidewall between the two illuminated. A projection from Devin's wrist gadget. Eddie realized what was happening.

The illuminated sidewall showed a live stream of a room captured from above. A bird's eye view. A man was sitting on an office chair. Three aliens, men in black uniforms, were around the chair. Two of them carried machine gun-like weapons. The same as the ones used by other guards at the atrium. Clearly, the third was the leader who was facing the captive. And possessed a sidearm on his belt.

"Speeak... How... did you... learn... our arrival... on this planet?" The leader asked the man in captivity. The sound coming through the ceiling was muffled. No doubt now, they are aliens, Thought Eddie. He watched the man on the shaky livestream. Devin had to curve his body to keep it stable between the two.

The leader squeezed the captive's mouth. The poor man screamed in pain. His hands were tied to the armrests of the chair.

"Tell mee... now. Other... wise..., we will... use more... aggressive... tactics. You... understand...?" The alien commander said. One of the guards slung his weapon on his shoulder and walked towards the nearest side table. He opened a large case and started to pull some cables. A screen popped up from the device. A device to make the captive talk thought Eddie.

"We can... drain... your memory. All ... of it. Understand?... It will not... be easy... for you," said the man, squeezing the detainee's face again. For a fraction of a second, the victim's face, disfigured in pain, turned upwards. Towards the ceiling where Eddie and Devin were.

"Fuck you. Is that me?" Eddie yelled. He completely forgot where they were. And the dire situation they were in.

Several things happened in the next instant. All three men, the aliens in uniforms, looked up at the ceiling. The confusion on their faces quickly changed to rage. The leader shouted something in his language, releasing the prisoner's face.

"Go back, go back, quick, quick, quick," Devin shouted while pocketing his wrist gadget. Suddenly, everything went dark. Eddie couldn't see anything. Then, his face was kicked by a pair of boots. Devin was already on the move backward. There's no point in moving silently anymore. Devin pressed his hands on the sidewalls and pushed his body towards Eddie, who was slow to respond in confusion.

With a squeaky noise, a light beam appeared two inches from Devin's nose. There was a perfectly circular hole in the metal sheet. Within a fraction of a second, several more openings and light beams appeared. The guards below were firing their weapons. The bullets continuously tore the ceiling around the two fugitives.

Eddie quickly realized the mistake he had just made. The momentary impulse he had ruined the opportunity to observe his future self. He couldn't understand what was going on below. Both himself and his future self are in danger at the same time. But there was no time to waste sorting the puzzle.

His head was already hit several times by Devin's boot. The guy was crawling backward furiously. Both were struggling to move away from the continuous barrage of bullets. Then, for a moment, the firing stopped.

"The wall," said Devin. "Before they come around to the next room, go back."

The two managed to backtrack to the central artery of the system. The squeaky noise of the alien weapons was heard below. But no bullet holes appeared closer to the two. Clearly, the aliens were shooting blindly.

Devin consulted his gadget once and started to move. Eddie tried to match his companion's speed. They heard shouting in the same unknown language. And the footsteps of guards running in the hallways. But no more firings.

They had to stop crawling Several times when they heard shouting directly below them. Devin didn't talk all the while they were wriggling in the narrow space. Instead, he was focused on the task ahead. Eddie blindly followed.

After around ten minutes, Devin stopped. The service tunnel entered a space where the two could comfortably sit. Devin spoke for the first time.

"We have to open this panel. There's a way to go out of the building." Frightened, Eddie didn't say anything. He has no other option.

Devin pulled a tool from his backpack. Tiny equipment blazed through the metal sheet with ease. Eddie sensed a faint, putrid smell. But that was the least of his concerns for the time being.

Devin managed to cut a square shape. The metal sheet dropped to the other side with a bang. He didn't show any concern. The entrance was barely enough for him to squeeze through.

"Go, go, quick. Those would be on our asses in a few minutes." He pushed Eddie first.

Going through the opening was not that hard. But the next part was. Eddie put his legs first. But the shoes didn't touch any surface. Before he realized he was on the ceiling, Devin forced him to the dark vertical shaft. In a few seconds, Eddie's legs met a hard surface. And his knees went limp. Before he regained composure, Eddie was hit by something heavy. Devin. And he dropped to the ground. A hard surface with a muddy, gluey texture. His face was covered with a smelly substance.

"Are you okay? Devin asked while standing up. "Congratulations, you jumped three stories."

He helped Eddie on his wobbly feet.

"Sorry, I didn't mean to jump on you. But we have to move." He switched on a light on his gadget.

"What is this place?" asked Eddie, trying to cover his nose with muddy hands.

"Don't worry. It is the waste disposal chute. It connects to the treatment plant near the river."

Devin took a flashlight from his backpack. That was enough to illuminate their way. It was an underground tunnel. And, straight like a railway line. The side walls and the ceiling had signs of old, white paint. The ground was muddy with black, gooey material and water. Both could walk comfortably in an upright position. At least that was a plus compared to crawling on a ceiling.

Devin ushered the way, almost like running. After around half an hour, he slowed and listened to his earpiece. Eddie silently watched the silhouette of his partner, panting. Suddenly, Devin pulled a tablet from his backpack. His pale face started to glow like a ghost.

"They are underground," he said without raising his head. Eddie saw red blotches on the otherwise black and grey screen.

"Need to change the plan." Devin marked some lines on the map, avoiding red patches.

Although Eddie had many questions, his partner was not in the mood for a conversation. They started to walk again. But at a much slower pace. The tunnel was quiet, except for the sloshing sounds they made with their boots. There were no signs of the pursuing black uniforms.

They walked for several hours, mostly in much smaller arteries, avoiding the main tunnels.

"Could there be aliens at the treatment facility? Eddie asked finally.

"Possible. But I don't think those buggers are that smart."

"Who are they? What do they want from me? I mean... future me."

Devin answered in one word. "Later."

"What the fuck? You dragged me into this mess. Why don't you tell me what's going on?"

"There's a time for everything. Let's get out of here first."

"No, you must tell me now." Eddie stopped abruptly. Like a disobedient kid. Ignoring him, Devin continued his stroll.

"Fuck you," shouted Eddie.

"They are aliens... from a different galaxy. One from far, far away. They would invade the earth if you didn't stop them now."

"What?" Eddie ran after his strange companion. "What did you say? They are like humans. Why did you say they are from a distant galaxy? How do you know? Tell me. Are you from there, too?"

Devin didn't answer. Instead, silently walked in his usual manner. Eddie pulled him by the shoulder. He stopped.

"Listen... It is more complicated than you think. You don't understand everything. There are humans in other galaxies. Far more advanced than earthlings."

Devin started to explain while walking. Eddie hurried beside his partner with an open mouth. It was straight out of science fiction. He wondered whether he was still drunk or dreaming. He felt wet, muddy water inside his shoes. It couldn't be an illusion. He had been walking with an alien for two days. A friendly one. And they were attacked by another group of extra-terrestrials.

Finally, the two managed to reach their destination without any glitches. There was no one to welcome Eddie and Devin. They exited the building without getting noticed by anyone. In fact, there was no one at the facility at the time. It was well past the sunset. The artificial moon was gradually increasing its glow, mimicking the real one.

The duo reached the bridge. A remnant from the past. For the first time in two days, Eddie saw trees. Since his arrival in the future. They crossed the river and started to walk under the tall cottonwoods. Eddie felt a vague familiarity with the surroundings. But he couldn't figure out what it was. The well-grown canopy obstructed the moonlight. Eddie turned back to face his companion. At that exact moment, he saw a movement from the corner of his eyes. Something dark. Moving through trees faster and towards him. In that instant, he realized that Devin was not there by his side. And the dark shadow ran past him, pushing his body to the ground.

When Eddie regained consciousness, he tasted blood. His gut started to churn with upward movement. He couldn't stop the rising pressure. At that moment of disgust towards the alcohol taste and smell, Eddie vaguely remembered what had happened. It was Friday night, and he was puking on the gravel road on his knees.

After several minutes of struggle, Eddie managed to stand up on his legs. He slowly walked towards the trailer park. To his satisfaction, the faint lights appeared at the end of the tree line.

But the next thing he saw puzzled him. His bike was lying in the middle of the road at the entrance to the trailer park. In the state of mind, he was in at the time, Eddie couldn't explain how it came there. He remembered he rode the bike when he had the accident.

#

Edmond McArthur walked into the cafeteria, which was full of staff members. Almost all of them respectfully acknowledged the entrance of their mayor. As usual, he waved to some people with a broad smile while walking towards the reserved table. A waiter quickly rushed towards the table.

"Good morning, Sir." He stood obediently beside the table with a nicely folded white linen on his arm.

"How are you doing today, Sam? It's a beautiful day, Isn't it?"

"Indeed, Sir... I'm doing fine. Thank you. The same order, as usual?"

"Yes, Sam. Thank you. Oh... make me a cup of coffee to take out, extra-large," Eddie replied while shuffling morning newspapers on the table.

Although printed newspapers are rare now, he always gets a glimpse of news in print every morning. Knowing his habit, the staff kept all newspapers on his table.

It didn't take long. Eddie came across the most terrifying item he never wanted to see again.

It was titled, *'Are aliens going to land in our city today, as predicted 25 years ago?'*

Eddie felt a chill along his spine. He vividly remembered the incidents he faced on a drunken Friday night. Exactly twenty-five years ago today. Also, he remembered how hard it was to decide to write that piece for his own newspaper. The most challenging part was to get the approval of his editor. Finally, the editorial board decided to publish his article as fiction. But it got the attention of readers across the state. Then, it went viral on digital media. Primarily because of the exact date and remarkable details of the aliens described in the article. Most of all, people like to learn that there are other humans in the universe. And we are not alone. Seeing the unexpected popularity, the editor asked Eddie to write a series expanding this concept. But he politely rejected the recommendation. He left the newspaper a few months later. And, most around him forgot his brief stint as a journalist.

Apparently, someone had found the long-forgotten article. And decided to remind the old story and the accurate predictions it made. Luckily, the editor had not given any prominence to that. It was tucked in the corner of a middle page. Most importantly, it was not linked to the mayor, Edmond McArthur. No one knew it was he who wrote the original article.

Exactly 25 years ago, our sister newspaper, Downtown Global, published an article foreseeing a possible alien landing in our city. A young and upcoming journalist, Edmond Nathan predicted that aliens would arrive on this day, September 17th. As the story goes, the aliens, a human race from a faraway galaxy, intend to invade the Earth. The author vividly illustrates the details of the extra-terrestrials and the advanced technology they possess. For an unknown reason, the advance party of the invaders arrives in our city.

Indeed, that's a long time, thought Eddie. He is not young anymore. Definitely not a journalist. After resigning from the newspaper company, he took the reins of his family enterprise. And quickly became successful and transformed the old business. Sooner, he eyed the politics. He's been serving as the mayor for twelve consecutive years. In recent months, He has been floating the idea of running for president within his inner circle of confidants. So far, he has received strong support. He intended to go public and launch his campaign within the next couple of weeks.

His streams of thought were disturbed by the approaching waiter. Sam carefully arranged the dishes on the table.

"Anything else, Sir?"

"No, Thanks." Eddie placed the paper on the table.

"Is that true, Sir? Are Aliens coming to the city today?" asked Sam with a mannerly smile. Eddie saw that the headline was staring at him.

"Oh... that's just a story. These journalists are crazy. They find something to make people worry."

"That's true, Sir. Most people are already worried after this news. It was on the TV, too."

Eddie almost choked his omelet. "What?... Was that on the TV?"

"Yes, Sir. On the morning news. Maybe after seeing this article."

Eddie felt anger rising inside. This could create many problems for him. If someone found that he was the one who predicted the alien attack, that could affect his presidential campaign. Maybe it is already out. But the immediate concern is to control the people. As an experienced politician, he knew what could happen next. Rumors like this are fodder for conspiracy theorists around the world. They can create chaos everywhere.

"Sam... I'll take my coffee with me," Eddie said, suppressing his emotions.

"Okay. Will bring it in a second, Sir."

Eddie gulped the remains on the plate while making a list of people to contact.

All the while, he could not suppress his thoughts on the possibility of the alien attack. Especially if he was what they were looking for as per his long-forgotten dream. He was the one who decided to publish the story. Now, it is coming back to haunt him at the most crucial time of his life. After all these years of space exploration, no one had found evidence of intelligent life elsewhere. That was the only relief he had for the last two decades. But, for ordinary citizens, one single news item is enough.

#

The day went by without any incident. The few calls he made in the morning worked well. Especially to a good friend who serves as the CEO of a major media network. Prominent scientists from NASA, the space force, and many other institutes were all over the TV channels, discussing the impossibility of alien attacks. The commander of the US Space Force, General Stephenson, guaranteed that there are no alien ships in the solar system or in our galaxy.

It was late afternoon, and Eddie decided to take a short break. He pressed a button on his intercom phone to call his secretary. There was silence. He shrugged and tried the cafeteria to order a cup of coffee. He got the same response. Eddie could not remember the last time their communication system had a breakdown. Maybe it never happened before. He decided to walk to the cafeteria.

Suddenly, his door opened with a bang. Three men rushed into the office. All in black uniforms, almost like combat suits. Involuntarily, Eddie dropped back to his seat. The next moment, he realized what was happening, with distant memories flowing through his mind. Eddie stayed staring at the short, muscular man in front of him. He felt sweat on his eyebrows and blood flowing into his cheeks.

This is real, Eddie thought. Instinctively, his eyes went toward the ceiling. And back towards the armed three in front of him.

The door was already closed. Eddie was alone with three strangers in his office room. None of them had any badges or insignia. Just plain black combat-like suits. Two guards walked around the table and stood by Eddie's sides. With their strange-looking weapons ready. The leader of the group sat on the chair facing the mayor.

"We... have a few... questions," the leader said with an unmistakable accent. And long pauses between words. Eddie realized how close it was to what he remembered from his weird experience a quarter century ago.

"Who are you?"

"We... are questioning... you. Not the... other way."

"You are unauthorized in this building. I'll call the police." Eddie touched his phone on the table. The man didn't say anything. Suddenly, Eddie remembered that the intercom didn't work a moment ago. These guys came prepared, thought Eddie.

"What do you want?" asked Eddie. He didn't want to show his vulnerability.

The leader pulled a piece of paper from one of his pockets. And slowly pushed on the table toward the mayor. The sight of that sent a chill along his back. *Aliens are real. They will be here on 17th September 2050.* The faded black letters were staring at him. The article he wrote twenty-five years ago.

"What... is the date...? That is... today... correct?" Eddie stayed silent, staring at the eyes of the alien. Pale yellowish eyes reminded him of snakes he had seen in movies.

"How... did you... know?" The leader leaned towards him over the table. "Who... helped you?"

One of the guards came closer behind him. Eddie realized what would happen next. He was debating whether he could change the sequence of events he knew.

Suddenly, he remembered the scene in the atrium. People on their knees and guards with their weapons aimed at them. The lives of his staff members should be at risk at this very moment. Unlike the last time, he knows all these people. As the mayor, he should be responsible for the lives of his citizens. Most of all, all this chaos is caused by his past actions.

"You are not aliens. What is this about?" He tried one last time.

"Don't... try to... fool us. We need... only one... answer. Who... told you?" The leader said, standing from his chair.

Then he mumbled something in a different language. At that moment, the door opened. Another uniformed guard brought a big metal case. The leader signaled him to place it on the side table. Eddie knew what it was. The apparatus to read the memory of anyone. He silently watched the guard and the box.

There's no escape now, thought Eddie. He tried hard to listen to any noise from above, hoping his old self and Devin would appear on the ceiling. Then he realized that he knew only up to that point. What would happen next? Would they kill him?

He decided to wait until the last moment. Until the two from the past show up on the ceiling. Then, he can decide whether to betray his strange partner for two days if necessary. Even though it was a distant memory, and he knew very little about Devin, he didn't want to put him in danger. But Eddie had no idea whether he was still alive.

"I don't know what you are talking about. I just wrote a story," said Eddie. Suddenly, the man in front of him rose from his seat while shouting. Two guards sprang to action. One held Eddie by his shoulder. The other took some metal straps from his pockets and placed them on Eddie's arms. It automatically wrapped around his arms together with the armrest of the chair. Eddie waited for the next moment, trying hard to hear any sound from the ceiling. But it never heard.

#

Eddie felt like a child in front of a giant dog. He is the most powerful man in the city. But utterly helpless and had surrendered to an unknown group of men. He blankly stared at his interrogator. The stocky leader held Eddie's face and stared directly into the eyes.

A few minutes ago, the two guards tied Eddie to his chair. One of them pushed a little plastic piece behind Eddie's neck. The sting was almost unnoticeable. He noticed the slight nod of the leader towards the subordinate. Obediently, the guy moved to the side table and started to work on the device.

For a few minutes, Eddie felt nothing unusual. Suddenly, he noticed some distant memories flooding his mind. Not particularly interesting incidents. But random events from the last fifty years. He stared absentmindedly at the alien leader standing in front of him. Once got clearance from the operator, he started to question Eddie.

"Who helped you?"

"Devin."

"Who is Devin?"

"I met him at the cemetery."

"Describe."

"Tall..., white as you guys..., had a scar on his face."

Eddie was not sure whether he was actually talking. He heard the questions in his head in perfect English. And answers flowed to his mind without any difficulty. All this time, Eddie was staring at the pale-yellow snake eyes in front of him.

Eddie's head started to ache. A slight pain started from the back of the neck and radiated toward the forehead. He felt blood warming his cheeks. All his intention was to cooperate with the man in front of him.

Suddenly, the door to his room opened. Three men, tall and heavily built, rushed with their weapons ready. This time, all three were in white metallic suits. In the next instant, men in black, including the alien leader, dropped to the ground. One of the men in white quickly ran towards the machine attached to Eddie and started to fumble with the controls. Although all these happened within a few seconds, Eddie felt like a slow-motion movie. Or he was high with a powerful intoxicant.

The two subordinates in white suits cleaned the room. Bodies of aliens and their machines were taken out. The room was, as usual, the Mayor's office again.

When Eddie regained consciousness again, he was on his office chair without the metal strains. He had no recollection of events that had happened in the preceding half an hour. A tall man in a white suit was sitting in front of him. His face was exceedingly familiar. The scar on the deathly white face was unmistakable. But Eddie could not remember where he had met him. The man stared at Eddie without any expression on his face. Like a marble statue.

Eddie silently watched his guest. Finally, the stranger broke the silence.

"Listen... you guys must ramp up your defenses against the aliens. There are more dangers out there than you can imagine," the long-haired man said. He slowly pushed the paper on the table towards Eddie. The same piece of paper that was presented by the alien leader earlier. The old newspaper article Eddie wrote twenty-five years ago. The one he wrote on a weird dream-like experience he had on a drunken night.

"Who are you? ...Why are you telling me?"

"My identity doesn't matter. I'm telling you because you are running for president," said the stranger and observed Eddie's puzzled face.

"You think aliens are real?" asked Eddie, wondering how this man knew about his plans.

"Why did you write this then?"

Eddie stared at him blankly. Somehow, he wanted to continue the conversation with this familiar stranger.

"Are you one of them?"

"You are not the only human race in this universe. There are many in the other parts. Countless galaxies are occupied. But not all of them are well-intentioned. Some are trying to invade habitable planets like this. Fortunately, or unfortunately, you are far away from the others. You must protect it from those aliens. It should be your priority in the next century or so." The stranger stood from his chair and had one last look at Eddie.

"We don't want to waste our investments on this planet. And we can't protect you forever." His last remarks were firm and authoritative.

Eddie observed the tall man leaving his office without any other word. Although he had many questions to ask, Eddie stayed silent, unsuccessfully trying to remember the face with a scar.

#

Mayor Edmond MacArthur entered the cafeteria to the standing ovation of his staff members. Everyone wanted to know how he predicted an alien attack a long ago. And eager to congratulate him on his presidential bid. Eddie smiled and shook the hands of a few people. He exchanged a few words with some who stayed around the closer tables.

The news broke the previous night by the commander of the US Space Force. The space force had intercepted an unoccupied alien vessel orbiting around the Earth. The investigations are still ongoing, and the government is expected to reveal more details soon.

The commander credited the secret mission they launched years ago for the swift actions. He didn't forget to mention the article Eddie wrote. Although it was a fiction published a long ago, the space force paid extra attention during this period. And stayed prepared.

Eddie walked through the crowd and reached his table. Sam was already there with a broad smile on his face. Ready to serve their mayor, potentially the next president. Eddie ordered his food and picked up the newspaper on the top of the pile.

'Protection of the earth from aliens is the priority,' says the presidential candidate, Edmond MacArthur. Reading the headline, Eddie smiled.

#

Somewhere in the asteroid belt, a tall man in a white metallic cloak firmly stood in front of a large screen. Long white hair was flowing over his shoulder. The dim lights from the screen exaggerated the deep scar on his face.

The display was divided into three equal sections. On the left was a planet in blue with its only satellite. On the right was a globe almost identical to the one on the left. But with two moons. The man waited until the image in the middle appeared.

A woman with long white hair sat on an extravagant chair. Her white cloak was decorated in gold. Her wrinkled face projected an aura of authority.

The man with a scar started communication. But his lips did not move. His eyes did not blink.

"The mission completed. The exploratory visit by the adversaries was successfully thwarted. The next leap in technological advances on the planet is already initiated. The monitoring mechanism is in place and functioning. No interventions are needed for now. Request permissions to start hibernation."

"Excellent," the ancient face nodded. "Permission granted."

#

Dan Chimsky

Space Traveler

Dan Chimsky

"What the hell is that?" Vivian whispered to himself, staring at the wall of monitors in front of him. His eyes have been glued to the screens for a few hours now. And his fingers have been dancing on the massive control panel. The command room wall was covered with several smaller computer displays around one large rectangle in the middle. Ceres was in the upper right corner of the middle screen. There were no other visible objects in the darker background. But, the asteroid, the biggest in the vicinity, was not what Captain Vivian Nippard focused on. The series of numbers and letters on one of the smaller screens.

The mining ship *Ekati* was cruising along the inner perimeter of the asteroid belt. It was named after one of the largest diamond mines on Earth. The Space Pioneers, the leading explorers of outer space, own a fleet of high-caliber ships. *Ekati* was one of the latest and largest models.

This was Vivian 's thirteenth mission as the captain of the behemoth. Their job was to extract M-type asteroids. And transport to Mars. Before being assigned as the captain, he had years of experience on other smaller vessels. To him, travel between Mars and the asteroid belt was like walking in his own backyard.

Vivian frantically typed to perform an extra analysis. The anomaly he detected a few hours ago seems to be an enigma. Something he has never seen in the asteroid belt.

"Jason, I need your help," Vivian said to his microphone.

"Yes, Captain. ...in a minute," came the swift reply.

Vivian didn't want to pull Jason, his only partner on the ship, from his off-shift rest. They have a busy day ahead. But this is urgent. Something is clearly off. The object Vivian noticed a few hours ago shows strange behavior. Instead of moving in an orbit like any other asteroid, it travels towards the center, towards the sun. Clearly a different beast.

While Vivian was still commanding the central computer to re-evaluate the path of the unknown object, the door to the cabin opened behind him.

"Captain?"

"Jason, get the telescope on these coordinates. We have a visitor there."

Jason Johnston, a veteran miner in the asteroid belt, immediately recognized the problem. The trajectory calculated by the machine didn't make any sense. He started to type even before sitting on the co-pilot seat.

The eyes of both astronomers were fixed on the digital wall while their fingers were swift at work.

"It is moving fast," said Vivian. "Definitely, not a boulder. It is coming towards us."

"I'm zeroing in... Will have a visual in a few seconds," Jason said.

The Ceres on the big screen started to move in the frame. Jason expertly maneuvered the joystick with his eyes on the pitch-black screen. A moment later, a tiny, grey dot appeared in the middle. Then, it slowly converted into a pixelated spaceship.

"That's it." Jason glanced at his captain and back at the visual feed. "Weird."

"See this projection. No doubt, it is going towards the Earth," said Vivian, staring at the screen. He mentally assessed the steps he went through. "Straight at it. No mistake. It is on a predetermined path."

"Reds?" asked Jason, looking at the worried face of his captain. He referred to the United Federation of Eastern

Earth. That is the only other jurisdiction on Earth. It has been at odds with the United States of the Western Hemisphere since the beginning of space explorations by humans. That started long before the two current coalitions were formed, where the Earth was politically divided into too many nations. And had two superpowers, one in the west and one in the east.

Although there was a peace treaty between the two governments, at least for space, minor conflicts occurred frequently. Both were eyeing mineral-rich profitable asteroids. Disputes on the ownership of some lead to clashes. Both parties have established fully functional colonies on Mars and Moon for the mining industry.

"Entirely possible," said Vivian, still examining the object on the screen. "But what is it? It seems too small for mining operations."

"And to be a surveying ship, too," added Jason.

"Definitely not a tin can." Vivian reminded the space junk. "The trajectory is too predictable. I did the simulation again."

"Should we inform the headquarters?"

"That's the law," said Vivian. "First, we'll try to figure out what it is. At this speed, it will take almost four-five months to reach the Earth. They have more than enough time to respond."

"Too slow for any of our ships. Even for red barrels," Jason said. The federation's mining vessels had an unusual shape, earning the nickname.

"That's the puzzle here. Our cargo ships are way faster than this."

"Could be aliens," said Jason jokingly.

Centuries of astronomical studies had ruled out the possibility of meeting extra-terrestrials in the solar system. Or in the vicinity.

"No doubt. It is coming from way beyond the belt. Most probably far out of the solar system."

#

"We haven't heard from the headquarters," Jason said.

The two on *Ekati* thoroughly studied the unusual object for the last few hours. No doubt it was a spacecraft sent from Earth. Probably centuries ago. One of the small ships designed for long-distance voyages, meaning beyond the orbits of planets and the Kuiper belt. Why it is coming back now is a mystery. Those early exploratory missions were designed to gather data. As long as they traveled through and beyond the solar system. Not to come back to the Earth.

Earlier, once confirmed the identity, Vivian relayed the information to the company headquarters on Mars. He specifically requested permission to contact the ship. To do that, *Ekati* must alter its current course and move toward the middle of the asteroid belt. Or wait until the mystery ship comes out of the area. It was painstakingly slow compared with modern spaceships. At the current speed, it would take days to make contact. That would delay the mining operations of *Ekati* by a long stretch.

"Isn't it unusual? I don't know why they take so long," Vivian replied. The only instruction they received so far was to monitor the mysterious ship.

"We should divert within the next couple of hours. Otherwise, we'll have to make a long loop. Or we should anchor here and wait until we get further instructions," said Jason. "Do you think we can catch it on our way back?"

"Yes, but... we will be with a full load," Vivian reminded. "We should go now. Or someone from Mars should come and meet it."

"Do you think there's any crew on that?" asked Jason.

"Hard to tell. There's no signal from the ship. None. But it is clearly programmed to reach the Earth."

"If there's any crew, all should be long dead. Or that could be one of the earliest with hibernation tech," suggested Jason.

"Yes. I've already informed that possibility. I wonder what it takes this long to issue any directive."

According to the space peace treaty between the two governments on Earth, it is the responsibility of the first spaceship to identify stray ships to rescue its crew. Provision of medical assistance if needed and transport personnel to the nearest colony is also mandatory. Failure to report a dysfunctional spaceship is a criminal offense.

All modern long-distance spaceships travel with a crew of suspended animation. Or commonly known as hibernation. Hence, it is the responsibility of the first ship to detect the dysfunctional unit to save the people sleeping in, oblivious to many dangers.

"Oh, my god. Did you see that?" shouted Jason. The central screen showed an enhanced image of the mysterious spaceship. "See the logo."

Then only Vivian noticed the smudged black patch on the whitish-grey background of the hull.

"Holy shit... Is that the big P?"

"Indeed," Jason typed on the keyboard. One of the smaller screens showed a digitally enhanced image. The logo and a series of letters and numbers below it. The large letter P had Earth in the middle. It was remarkably similar to the current company trademark. Both knew the symbol changed throughout history, but without losing its identity.

Pioneer Blue was one of the earliest space exploration companies on Earth. In fact, Space Pioneers was established after the amalgamation of several smaller companies with Pioneer Blue. That was nearly two hundred years ago.

"We have no choice. We should go now."

Vivian punched the keys of the control panel. It takes only a few minutes to transfer data to the headquarters on

Mars. "Whatever its mission was, that is one of ours. We better rescue it first."

#

Sheila Patel was fully immersed in her work. Urgent analysis of data received from *Ekati,* their largest mining ship. Her orders were clear. That was the utmost priority for the day. But she did not expect it to be digging into the history of the company.

There is a handful of data scientists, including Sheila, in the headquarters. Usually, they are busy identifying steroids for extraction. The fleet of thirty-odd ships sends copious amounts of data on probable asteroids for future mining. Since the mining ships extract whole asteroids and transport them to Mars, size is one of the main criteria. Then, of course, the economic value. Their main targets are manageable M-type asteroids that are rich in precious metals. Occasionally, the ships extract modest C-type asteroids if identified as diamond-rich rocks.

It is uncommon for data scientists to work on stray spacecraft. That is a job for the Space Force operating from the Earth. Not for a commercial venture like Space Pioneers.

But, when Sheila received the images, she gasped in disbelief. She knew her spaceships very well. At first glance, Sheila realized how ancient this ship could be. That is a job for an Astroarchaeologist, she thought.

"How old are you? Pioneer Blue was in operation in that name more than two centuries ago." Sheila murmured to herself. She looked at the image of big P. And copied the letters and numbers below the logo. Her fingers typed SP25-00.

The central database of Space Pioneers contained all the data from its inception. That includes Pioneer Blue and other incorporated companies as well. More than a couple of thousand spaceships have been in operation for the period.

The search came empty again.

"What? ...No spacecraft?"

She decided to go year by year. The year 2025 came with one name, SP25-01. No ships were launched in the next two years. SP28-01 in the year 2028. Another two were sent in 2029, promptly named SP29-01 and SP29-02. And two ships the year after. The pattern was clear as water. At the time, the names of the spaceships were assigned based on the year with a sequel number.

"What the hell is SP25-00 then?" Sheila murmured to herself while requesting another query.

Today, time is not on her side. Captain Vivian is already bugging her for a quick response from the command center. She understood his urgency. But she was stuck here.

Searches in a couple of old dormant databases came fruitless as well. There's only one place to find information on early space missions of the Earth. The archives of the Space Force. But it needs special permission from the authorities. It will take at least two days to clear the bureaucratic hurdles on Earth. But *Ekati* cannot wait that long. Besides, SP25-00 is a property of the company. There should be information somewhere, even if it was a coveted mission.

Suddenly, Sheila realized to whom she should talk. Mr. Benjamin Graham, vice chairman of the company. He is one of the oldest living members of the Graham family, the founders of Pioneer Blue. He was born on Mars long after the company became Space Pioneers. But, Benjamin is a walking library with a vast knowledge of space history. Besides, he is the uncle of the current CEO, Deon Graham.

Sheila called Benjamin and explained the situation. She also transferred the images of the mystery ship she received from *Ekati*.

"Sheila, thank you for sending those images. I have never seen anything like that. I will look into it and get back to you soon."

"But, Sir..., the problem is whether this carried humans. If so, *Ekati* should rescue them. It is already on the verge of passing maneuverable region."

"I know, I know... It won't be that long. I'll call the Earth and get back to you."

Sheila didn't think that went well. Benjamin's manner of responding puzzled her. He usually is the friendliest high-ranking officer in the headquarters. Sheila regretted calling a big boss of the company, fearing that would affect her career.

In less than five minutes, her computer chimed. And signaled an emergency meeting. A highly classified one. Her eyes went to the closed door in her cubicle. No one was around. When she prompted, Deon Graham, the CEO, appeared. Something she had never expected. Oddly, the young businessman was attired in casual outfits. Clearly, he is enjoying a vacation somewhere tropical on Earth. The camera of his portable device showed lush green trees and a bright blue sky in the background.

"Sheila," the CEO addressed by her first name. "Benjamin updated me. I will contact Captain Nippard right away. Don't worry about that. Transfer all data received from *Ekati* into the classified vault. No one else, other than you, should see it. Okay?" Sheila blankly stared at the screen, not understanding what was going on.

"Only you and Benjamin know about this. So, keep it that way."

"But sir...," Sheila struggled. "Don't we need to report it to the Space Force?"

"No. We'll keep it under wrap for now. It's one of ours anyway. Do you understand?"

Sheila nodded, looking at the unsmiling face. The screen went blank.

#

Vivian was enraged at his command center on Mars.

"What the hell is going on? This is really unusual. Why can't they send some instructions? They have all the data," Vivian said while studying the image on the central display. Now, they have a much better, enhanced visual on the screen.

"I wonder why it doesn't emit any signal. No radio signals, No IR laser, ...nothing. Isn't it the standard in early spaceships?" asked Jason, partly to calm down his captain.

"Yes, but this is really old. Don't think most of the ship is functional after all these years."

"At least some parts are working. It has clear directions to return to Earth."

"Yes, That's true."

Suddenly, the control panel chimed, signaling an incoming message. When prompted, the relic spaceship on the big screen jumped to a smaller one on the left. And the main space was filled with an image of a young, bald man in a white t-shirt. Not Sheila Patel, as the duo expected. Both Jason and Vivian involuntarily stood from their seats. Astronauts do not receive instructions from their CEO every day. The dense, green vegetation in the background was clearly somewhere tropical.

"Captain," Deon Graham started without any introduction. "Your mining mission is aborted with an immediate effect." It was a decision of a few billion dollars. But there was no hint of emotions on his face.

"Retrieve the old spaceship right away. And return to the company loading deck... lightspeed. By the way, don't report to the space force. Understood?".

"Yes, Sir," said Vivian.

"Secure the ship in the cargo bay as it is. Don't mess with it." The CEO said with an unwavering tone. "And... do not communicate with any other ship. Remember..., This is a highly classified mission. From now on, communicate directly with me... No one else. You have an open channel. Understood?"

"Yes, Sir," said Vivian, standing still in front of the wall of monitors.

The CEO nodded, and the screen went black. In an instant, SP25-00 jumped back to the central screen.

"What the hell is going on? ...why the bald man is in command now?" Jason looked at his captain.

"I don't know, man... Something is clearly off." Vivian said, shaking his head. "Have you ever heard a mining ship suspended its operations mid-air?"

"True," Jason agreed. "For some reason, that junk should be worth more than the billion-dollar boulder we were going to pull. Otherwise, the CEO won't call us."

"For the first time in my life in the space, I'm engaged in an illegitimate operation," Vivian said, taking his eyes off the screens. "I don't understand why we must keep this from the government."

"At least the Space Force can't detect us at this range. I don't think they are in this part of the belt. Thankfully, they have enough on their plates with the Reds," said Jason, studying the screens. "How do you want to do this? ...loop around it?"

"Yes, it is flying towards the center. We must go around. We'll pick it up on our way back. We would have more than enough juice to go back to Mars."

"Okay, I'll take over from here. You can take a rest, captain."

"Thanks, Jason. It will take a few hours at max speed. Let's do it at ninety. No need to push this beast to the limits."

Jason took the helm and started maneuvering *Ekati*, the mining ship. Vivian went to the sleeping cabin next door to rest after several hours of indecision. He had never extracted a spaceship before. Picking asteroids from space is easy. No need to worry about any damage to the object. Once commanded, the robotic arm gently pulls boulders toward the cargo bay. It is as simple as picking a pebble from the ground. Once inside, massive rocks are automatically strapped to the floor. That helps to avoid unnecessary movements during the flight and landing on Mars. But this task is entirely different. They need to make sure there is no damage to the ancient ship.

Vivian was still puzzled. Why did the CEO ask to abort the mining mission? *Ekati*, the largest of the company, has enough space in the hull. Their target was not a full load this time. They could easily accommodate both SP25 and their bounty. *Ekati* would not be any slower, even with its maximum load capacity. It seemed that the CEO didn't want to wait an extra day.

While trying to have a nap before the task ahead, Vivian wondered whether the CEO would be on Mars to welcome the relic ship.

#

Dr. John McNeil examined the sleeping pod still attached to the SP25-00, the ancient spaceship found among asteroids. A young man with jet-black hair was lying inside the pod. His skin was tight and fresh. John was amazed by the lively look of the gentleman, probably not even forty. But, if he could wake up from deep slumber, he would be centuries old. It was a miracle, even at today's standard.

Five days ago, John received a call from Mr. Deon Graham. The CEO offered him an unimaginable compensation package for an assignment of one week. It was a fortune compared to his annual income as a university professor. And only for one week on Mars. Without hesitation, he blindly accepted the lucrative offer. He knew very few details about the project. But it was not inconceivable.

John was the prime authority on suspended animation research. His studies with the collaboration of the space force on human space hibernation were ground-breaking. However, he never expected to bring a two-hundred-year-old man to life.

Within five minutes of acceptance of the offer, John was picked up at his office at the university. He was out of the Earth's atmosphere in the next hour. It was so swift John didn't get a chance to pack even clothes for the tour. He traveled with Deon Graham, the CEO of the Space Pioneers, in a company shuttle.

During their two-day trip to Mars, Deon explained the situation. Since it was a highly secretive mission, only John was assigned to work on the ancient spaceship. No assistants. He had to sign a non-disclosure agreement for life.

John spent the next two days on the shuttle, studying two hundred years old data provided by Benjamin. According to the Vice-chairman, the records were curated in a family archive. That was in an ancestral house on the Earth. Only a handful of family members knew about the existence of those files. None of the living relatives expected to open the archive in their lifetimes. But now, the time has come.

On Mars, once landed, the mining ship *Ekati* was directed to a quiet corner of the company premises. Farther away from the central biosphere. The Space Pioneers has a landing dock on their own. That provided trouble-free arrivals and departures without any government intervention. Since the company initiated the Mars colonization project long ago, it has a sizeable chunk of habitable space on the red planet.

Once landed, *Ekati*'s two astronauts were immediately sent to Earth for a six-month paid vacation. When they arrived on Mars, a company shuttle was ready for Vivian and Jason at the same landing port. Sheila Patel was already onboard, leaving for her retreat as well.

In the next two days, the cargo bay of *Ekati* was converted into a sophisticated lab. John was amazed by the speed of the developments. In the end, he had a much better lab with all the necessary facilities. Once completed the arrangements John was the sole occupant. However, Deon and Benjamin visited him to oversee his progress.

The scientist was still uncertain about the correct procedure to resurrect the founder of Pioneer Blue. He had thoroughly studied the given instruction. Those were written on a gold plate and attached to the sleeping pod. According to current standards, those techniques are outdated. John knew those were the methods developed by early scientists. That was the early stages of the hibernation experiments. Procedures have changed drastically since then.

Space travel was still at infantry in the early twenty-first century. However, there were ambitious plans to establish a colony on Mars. At the time, the most advanced spaceships took more than nine months to travel to Mars from the Earth. The idea of suspended animation, or space hibernation, was around for a while. Mainly to cut the excessive energy needs of the crew onboard. But the experiments on humans were at a very primitive stage. John had no clue, until five days ago, that a human subject was hibernated that early. And sent to outer space. First published reports, as far as he knew, appeared several decades later than the launch of this ship. Now he knows why.

During the last two centuries, hibernation technology has advanced in leaps. The current techniques are much faster and cheaper. Most importantly, those are reliable and less risky. However, John had trouble deciding whether to use the currently accepted methods or the one written on the pod.

He didn't want to risk the life of two-hundred-year-old Roland Graham. The first man to travel beyond Mars. And in suspended animation. For John, this is an opportunity of a lifetime. No one has ever studied the physiology of a human body hibernated for such a long time.

While John was still working on the sleeping pod, the door to the cabin opened.

"How are you doing, John? Any progress?" asked Deon. He came with his uncle Benjamin to examine the process.

"Just finished plugging supplies. First, we need to raise the oxygen levels slowly. Currently, it's at a dangerously low level. Luckily, we found it early. If we waited until it comes back to Earth, it could be too late," said John, pointing to the sleeping young man. "Don't think he had enough amounts to visit Earth. That would be unfortunate if he couldn't survive after this long journey... at the cusp of his return."

"So, he is alive?" asked Benjamin, carefully examining the face of his ancestor through the curved, thick glass. Deon watched his uncle bend down to observe Roland's face with amusement.

"Of course... he is very much alive. His heart rate is at four beats per minute. You know... that is a great achievement for scientists at the time. Metabolic rate at ten percent. Remarkable."

"Would it take long to wake him?" asked Deon.

"That's what I'm debating. We can use our latest tech to wake Mr. Roland within an hour. The methods they used at the time and suggested on this pod take at least forty-eight hours." John pointed towards the gold plate attached to the side panel of the sleeping pod.

"Do it as fast as you can," suggested Deon, looking at his uncle.

"Why do we rush? Let him decide the best," said Benjamin.

"Do you have any idea why he did this? What was the plan?" John asked the elder one in the room.

"Everyone knew he was a kind of crazy character. Crazy enough, now we have a colony on Mars. And on other planets as well. The simple answer is he wanted to be the first man to travel into deep space, beyond the solar system," said

Benjamin, smiling. He understood the family trait of extreme risk-taking very well as one of the descendants himself.

"At the time, our technology was at a very primitive stage. People laughed at him for starting Pioneer Blue. A space exploration company. The first of that kind. But he had a vision... and a mission. Look now. It is the largest space mining company. He pushed his scientists on two things. First, better, faster, and more reliable spaceships. The other is space hibernation. He achieved both. That was the origin of the current era of space travel."

"But why did he want to experiment with himself?" John asked.

"That's how crazy he was. He accomplished everything when he was forty. As you already know, his travel was a top-secret mission. Only a very few in the company were aware of it. Not even the immediate family, until he was out of Mars' orbit. The media reported he was missing on a trip to Amazon. Rainforests of the south on Earth. But, in fact, no one knew about the launch of this ship. Partly because of the government regulations at the time. This was hidden inside a much larger spaceship and launched later into outer space," said Benjamin, admiring his ancestor sleeping in the pod.

"So, what was his idea? ...Travel indefinitely?"

"That... no one knows. Roland had planned everything with utmost secrecy. I assume his idea was to travel away from the solar system... As far as he could. ...probably expecting some other intelligent species would find him someday. But there are some rumors in the family that he took something important. Maybe something valuable. But no one knows what that is. It's just a story."

"Where was it heading? Does data from the ship suggest anything?" asked John, turning to face Deon.

"We are still analyzing its data. But initial reports suggest it was headed in the general direction of the Centaurus cluster. Probably towards the Proxima."

"How far do you think it went?"

"Don't know yet. By the capacity of the ship and the time since the launch, it must have reached the Oort cloud," said Deon, proudly looking at his ancestor. The only person in human history to travel that far.

"But... then why did the ship come back? Wasn't it traveling towards the Earth when discovered in the asteroid belt," asked John.

"Yes. But we don't know why exactly it turned back. My instinct is that it could be a gravity-assist maneuver... Happened in or beyond the Kuiper belt. There are many large objects in the Kuiper. And many detached objects like Sedna beyond the belt. We already know some are large enough to provide sufficient gravitational force. Small ships like this can easily swing by around those. But the problem is one of those events would not turn it complete one-eighty," Deon explained.

"Can we find it using data from the ship?"

"Possible. It will take a few days to get a complete picture. We are working on it."

Benjamin, who was silent for a while, joined the conversation.

"There is something else. There was a family archive we were not allowed to open until this week. Those were some printed materials. Sealed two hundred years ago in our repository. According to those files, the lead scientist, Doctor

Phillip Green, had built a failsafe into the plan. In fact, without knowledge of Roland. It is possible when the ship was misdirected, the failsafe was triggered. And this little vessel started the return journey." Benjamin paused for a moment. And observed his ancestor's face. "Probably, when the onboard resources are diminished. I guess Phillip knew the limitations of his technology at the time. That's the maximum time he could keep his boss alive in this ship."

"So, Phillip had acted against the last will of his master?" John asked.

"Seems like that. Dr. Greene sealed all the information. However, he included his narrative as well."

"Do you think Roland has something important? Inside the pod or in this ship? Is that why you keep this a secret from the government?" John turned to Deon again.

"I don't think so. It's just a rumor. A bedtime story for kids in the family. We scanned the whole ship for anything unusual. Nothing," Deon replied dismissively. "The problem is... we might face penalties if the government learned that the company launched a ship without permission... Even two centuries ago... even under a different company name. So, we need to keep this a secret until we learn more. Let's see what Roland has to say." Deon stared at the body. He felt weird to see this young man as his great-grandfather by seven generations.

"Okay... let me know when he is waking up. I want to be here," said Deon.

#

The mood in the situation room was grim. Everyone was waiting for the arrival of the President. All the security council members, except one, were present. The only absentee was the Commander of the Allied Forces of Mars. General Sadik Ivanovich was not expected to attend physically. However, the dedicated screen for his long-distance appearance was empty. The heads of all armed force units on Earth and the moon flew to the President's office on short notice. The classified briefing they received earlier did not elaborate on the situation on Mars. Everyone knew something was terribly wrong. And it could be everyone's problem very soon.

"Good morning. Let's start this," President Idris Dos Santos said while entering the room. His chief of staff closed the door behind him as the President hurried toward the head table. All thirty-three generals went silent, ready to listen. Defense Secretary Retired General Colin MacArthur looked at his colleagues around the table and the President on his left.

"Mr. President... as I already briefed, the situation on Mars is out of control... far worse than we thought earlier. According to the latest information I received five minutes ago, almost two-thirds of the population in our colony is dead. We prohibited all travel to and from Mars as of yesterday. People who traveled to Earth and Moon within the last week are isolated and quarantined. Luckily, they are all healthy so far. No signs of any infection," the defense secretary updated the assembly.

"Any update on the cause?" President asked, observing the gloomy faces of his generals.

"I talked to the chief medical officer there this morning. The reports suggest that everyone died of heart failure... At least all the bodies the health officials could examine so far. Strangely, there were no other comorbidities. And, none had prior conditions of concerns," the defense secretary continued.

"As we all know, Martians are healthy. Healthier than our population on Earth. But it is clear... this is caused by a virulent germ... most probably a virus. Scientists are struggling to find the exact agent. But no success so far."

"What is the exact date of onset?" asked General Henry Makela, the Commander of the Allied Forces of Moon.

"The first person died three days ago at the mining facility of Space Pioneers. In fact, a bunch died within a couple of hours that day. Almost all of their staff on Mars is deceased by now... Including the CEO." The defense secretary looked at the President. He knew about the close connection between the President and Deon Graham.

"The current working hypothesis is that the germ entered the biosphere through a spaceship. Space Pioneers has a busy spaceport. On average, five mining ships from outer space land every week. Mostly from the asteroid belt. And numerous shuttles from Earth and moon."

"But...," General Makela started to protest.

"The mining ships... Don't they process their cargo outside the central biosphere?" asked the President, silencing his General.

"Yes, Sir. That's the puzzle here. The processing unit is completely isolated. Most operations do not need human intervention. It's fully automated. None of the materials they collect from the asteroid belt don't enter the biosphere. Even the staff at the plant enters the living quarters after a rigorous quarantine process," said the defense secretary.

"Could it be an infiltration of Reds?" asked General Kalil Thorsden, Commander of Europe and Near East. His region has the only shared land border with the United Federation of Eastern Earth, the Reds. Everyone in the room is well aware of the capabilities of their only nemesis. The cold war between the two governments has a history that goes far beyond the inception of the two federations a hundred and fifty years ago.

"That's a real possibility. But you all know. The security of our biosphere is tight. There are no records of any breach. We are going through all the logging records, as far back as three months. No suspicious entry of Reds or any known associate," said General MacArthur.

The discussion went on for another half an hour. But most of that was elaborations from the defense secretary. Other members of the council wanted to know more about the situation. Most generals were suspicious of a covert operation by the Reds. The main reason was that their colony on Mars was unaffected. At least, there were no reports of any disturbance in their biosphere so far. A few generals supported the idea of issuing a warning to the Federation. The President observed the animated discussion without any comments.

"This is a total failure... A shame. Our whole population on Mars is almost wiped out. But we don't know what caused it. Without any evidence, we can't start a war against the Federation. We need a solution... Not now. Yesterday." The President voiced his concerns at last. "There's no point in arguing without clear evidence of an attack. Tell me, ...What should we do now. We need swift action."

"Sir, the Earth is safe for now. And the moon and all other space stations. As long as there are no contacts with Mars. We have travel restrictions in place. We are monitoring everyone who came from Mars within the last two-week period. This..., whatever it is, spreads like wildfire. If anyone is infected, they should show signs by now. I mean dead," said the defense secretary. "Sir... A team of medical professionals is waiting for your authorization to travel. They can reach Mars by tomorrow evening local time if they leave within the next hour."

"Any objections?" The President looked at the expressionless faces of his generals. "Okay, send them immediately."

The defense secretary handed over the documents to sign. While the President was signing, the communication system chimed.

"General Sadik...," said the secretary, looking at the President. He nodded to connect with the man who was the center of attraction at the time. The officer with a tired face appeared on the screen. General Sadik Ivanovich was in his field uniform. A stark contrast to the decorated uniforms of other officers in the room. It was apparent to everyone that he had a long, busy day.

"Mr. President... my apologies for the delay. This is totally out of control now. We are running out of staff to run the biosphere. Don't think anyone would survive at the end of tomorrow."

"I'm really sorry, Sadik. I understand the situation there. Any progress on finding the cause of this pandemic?" asked the President.

"One of the mining ships of Space Pioneers had extracted an ancient vessel from the asteroid belt. An early spaceship launched from the Earth long ago, two centuries, to be exact. A secret mission launched by the mother company of Pioneers. We have credible reports that it contained a hibernated body."

"Oh, that's why Mr. Graham left Earth suddenly, abandoning his vacation?" said the defense secretary, looking at his data pad.

"Yes, and he arrived here with Dr. John McNeil, who is specialized in human hibernation technology. Both are dead now."

"Have they resurrected the body? That should be impossible. Isn't it?" asked the President.

"We believe... yes, Mr. President. A search operation is underway. If he is still alive, he must be in the central biosphere. There's no sign of life in the mining facility. I'll update the progress as soon as possible."

"Any idea what causes these heart failures?" asked the President.

"This is just out of the oven. I've just got this from our medical team. That's why I waited to connect," said General Ivanovich, looking at his data pad.

"It looks like a virus... an airborne vector. Strangely, it stays only an hour or so in the human body. Apparently, that's enough time to replicate and spread. For some reason, we rarely find traces of it in dead bodies. Probably, the virus can't survive the inner body temperatures." General Ivanovich stopped for a moment. No one in the room said anything, expecting more from him. "Here is the strangest part. The team discovered an unknown prion on the cardiovascular centers of the brain. They suspect a possible connection between the prion and the virus."

"What?" General Juliet Krausse almost screamed. "That is simply impossible."

She has a doctorate in virology and is the head of the Medical Research Institute of the United Armed Forces. She was specially invited to this extraordinary meeting of the security council. Everyone, including the President, looked at her outburst. Before she protested again, General Ivanovich addressed the gathering.

"I know... I know... My team informed me of the improbability of such a thing. But that is the only explanation we have for the moment. The med team believes this prion probably comes with the viruses. A symbiotic pair. Or it is a byproduct of the replication process. Again, we need more research. Unfortunately, we have no time. And I am out of qualified staff.

"Pass that information to the squad going there. And Julie's team here," said the President. He knew the crew could already be in space, traveling fast to Mars. Even though he authorized it a few minutes ago.

#

Roland leaned against the metal fence of the observation deck. He savored the magnificent view of the central biosphere below. A massive swath of green, interrupted by a few sporadic buildings, in front of his eyes was indeed a miracle. A large majority of the living spaces were built underground. Almost all the ground surface, except for a few structures, was covered with crop plants. And some areas with ornamental trees. Recreational parks for the residents. Everything is inside a gigantic glass bubble.

As a young scientist, he envisioned the Mars project more than two centuries ago. But when he was in his twenties. At the time, everyone laughed at him. No one thought it was technically feasible and, moreover, economically viable.

Nevertheless, he formed Pioneer Blue with a long-term plan of colonizing the red planet. The initial designs were for a much smaller biosphere. A bare minimum for the operations at the time. Obviously, it was built upon the one he designed himself. And the central biosphere he was in now, with some modifications to his plans. Unfortunately, he was long gone when living on Mars became a reality. The first few manmade structures on the planet are still preserved inside the biosphere. Now, expanded to a massive scale, the colony has a separate government on Mars.

One of the major obstacles at the initial stage was the time taken to travel between Earth and Mars. It took at least nine months to reach the red planet. That is, only if they carefully planned the launch, considering the orbital positions of the two planets. Under his direction, scientists at Pioneer Blue worked on two fronts. First, developing better, faster spaceships. At the time, almost all space shuttles were launched using chemical propulsion. Although the idea was not new, nuclear thermal propulsion was not practically possible. For the Mars colonization project, he needed massive vehicles that cruise fast. And with a bigger capacity to transport construction materials. Hence, their priority was to develop nuclear-powered ships.

His second goal was to expand the technology on human suspended animation. He didn't plan to stop at Mars. To explore beyond the red planet, even with faster ships, astronauts need better living facilities. And more advanced traveling conditions.

A broad smile came to Roland's face, remembering his team's achievements. At the time, space hibernation was restricted only to science fiction. Even the best research institutes were reluctant to engage in such experiments. But, against all odds, he managed to gather a team. His long-time friend, Dr. Phillip Greene, led the experts. Roland reminded himself how excited he was when the initial results were shown to him. That was when he picked the interest in traveling to infinity. To be the first man to travel beyond the solar system. To the interstellar. To meet extra-terrestrial life somewhere in the universe. To be the lab rat himself for an advanced lifeform someplace.

Memories flooded him while Roland was scanning the biosphere. At the same time, he was amazed by his memory. His ability to remember the details of his past. Even after two centuries. He recalled how he planned everything with Phillip, the only person to know about his disappearance. First, the faithful scientist vehemently rejected the idea. Because the technology was still untested and at a very primitive stage. Only a handful of human subjects had been experimented with. And only for a maximum of one year in deep sleep. Moreover, none was tested in space, outside the Earth's atmosphere. Everything was done in his research facility in the Canadian Arctic.

But Roland was firm on his decision. He had already transferred the majority of company responsibilities to his younger brother, Harry. Finally, Phillip agreed to do what his life-long friend asked for. The spaceship SP25-00 was hidden inside another experimental ship. It was one of the largest ships launched by humans to that date. Even the company staff didn't know about the departure of their CEO onboard. Phillip secretly arranged the initiation process of hibernation in the sleeping pod.

Roland was already in deep slumber when the ship left the company launch pad. The SP25-00 was ejected into outer space, halfway through Earth and Mars. On the sidelines, Roland planned an excursion to South American rain forests and of his own disappearance.

Everything went according to the plan except for one. Roland learned what that was only a few days ago. Only when he woke up from his two hundred years of sleep. Deon informed him about a possible failsafe mechanism built into the ship. That could probably turn the vessel back towards Earth. Roland felt mild anger towards his long-dead friend, Phillip.

Roland silently observed the biosphere below. Although the area was covered in trees and shrubs, he knew it was a lifeless colony below. Every one of his kind is dead. He felt a chill along his back. He was responsible for it. Only himself is to blame. No one else.

Two of his descendants, the only living relatives he knows, died two days after his resurrection. And Dr. John McNeil, who looked after his rebirth. One by one, people around him started to die mysteriously. First, the Space Pioneers company employs at the mining facility. Then, it spread into the central biosphere. He understood what exactly was happening. He was the one who initiated the deadly pandemic. But the puzzle was why is he still alive.

Roland tried to think of possible causes. Something was nagging him. But he couldn't figure out what it was. He looked up at the glass ceiling. The sky was dark. No stars or moon. The lights inside the bubble obscured the dim radiations of the distant stars. He started to fantasize about his return trip awaken. What would he observe from his small spaceship? Would he recognize the colony on Mars from a distance?

Suddenly, it clicked. Roland remembered a weird dream he had while hibernating. The only one he thought he had during that time.

Roland did not know when. At one point, he started to wake up. And heard a few standing around him talking. But he didn't understand their dialect. A foreign language. Groggily, he opened his eyes. He saw silhouettes of human shapes around his bed. Four or five. He tried to open his eyes and focus. Those around him came closer. They all had uncharacteristically pale skin. All were in black uniforms. One of them bent down and did something around his neck. He felt a pinch of a needle. Seeing two pale yellowish irises on him, Roland felt a chill. And he went back to his slumber again.

Roland played the dream again and again. He tried to think whether it actually happened. His hand involuntarily went to his neck. But there was nothing. He tried hard to recall what he was missing. Then he remembered what was forgotten. For a fraction of a second, he saw the central display of the control panel from his sleeping pod. One black uniform was standing in front of it. On the screen was the blue planet. The Earth.

He wanted to inspect his ship. To see if there's anything he can find. Roland started to stroll towards the elevator. Suddenly, a speaker crackled somewhere close to him.

"Mr. Roland Graham... This is President Idris Dos Santos. The President of the United States of the Western Hemisphere on Earth." The speaker addressed directly to Roland. During his first two days on Mars, he learned about the political structure on Earth and other colonies. So, he knew who was addressing him. And why.

"Mr. Graham..., first of all, welcome back to civilization. And congratulations on your incredible journey," said the President. Roland wondered whether he was being watched.

"Mr. Graham, Deon, your great-grandson..., whatever the relationship is, was a good friend of mine. Unfortunately, he is dead at this young age. You know what's happening around you. According to our reports, you are the only living human being in our colony on Mars now." There was silence for a moment. Roland felt the weight of that statement.

"Yes, that's right. All our citizens are dead from a mysterious disease. According to the information I received, it appeared after your arrival. Listen..., I don't blame you, Roland. It's not your fault. We were not prepared. Simple as that. We have never expected such a thing in the colony," the President said. Roland stayed silent, staring at the speaker on the wall. It was not a two-way communication.

"But there's a bright side," said the President. And paused for a moment. "First, Earth and other outer space settlements are safe. At least for the time being. Second, and most important. Strangely, this highly infectious germ did not affect you. You are perfectly healthy, even after a two-hundred-year sleep. And a long journey. It suggests that you are immune to this virulent germ. We believe you can help us to understand this disease. And eliminate it forever. We know that you are the pioneer of the space exploration of what we have today. We asked you to help us once again." Roland felt the desperation in the President's tone.

"Mr. Graham, we have better facilities on Earth for such studies. So, we prepared everything for your return to Earth. There is an unmanned shuttle at the Space Pioneers' landing port. It is programmed to arrive here... with all the necessary precautions. You don't have to do anything. Once inside, it will automatically start the voyage. I know you understand the situation. Please, help us to save humanity." The speaker went silent.

#

Roland arrived at the biosphere of Space Pioneers. It was a much smaller half-dome compared to the central biosphere. And separated from it. But connected through an underground tunnel. Three enormous cargo ships, including *Ekati*, were parked beside the mineral processing plant. Passenger shuttles from the Earth are stationed at a smaller landing strip with a direct access terminal to the biosphere.

Roland observed the parking bay through the curved glass walls. There were three small shuttles. Two of them he already knew. One was the ship Deon and Benjamin used for their personal travel. It was there since Deon's sudden arrival on Mars a few days ago. Roland had the opportunity to examine the ship on his first day on Mars.

Then, there was SP25-00. Deon wanted to learn more about ancient technology. Hence, he advised his team to restore it. Thanks to the dedicated team of scientists, it was launch-ready in a day.

There was a third vessel parked beside SP25-00. It was similar to Deon's personal shuttle by size and design. But with a different color scheme. It had a colorful logo painted on the trunk and words below it. The Space Force of the United States of the Western Hemisphere. That's his ride to the Earth. Roland suspected a crew had arrived to examine the damage.

Roland walked inside the access ramp. At the end of the tunnel, the path divides into three, towards the three spaceships. He hesitated at the intersection. He was still struggling to decide what to do next. His extraordinary actions helped humanity to advance in space technology in leaps. That was in the past. But his recent arrival on Mars wiped out all living human beings. The dream of his life, the one he had built the foundation, collapsed because of himself.

He has two paths open in front of him. One, go to the Earth, where he was born and lived all his life. And help the authorities to find a cure for this mysterious disease. But what if they are not capable of containing it. Roland didn't want to see the same fate happen to the population on Earth.

The other option is to continue his unfulfilled journey toward the infinity of the universe. His ship SP25-00 is ready again with his sleeping pod. Now, with more advanced technology.

Roland looked back at the ramp he walked. Then at the two paths in front of him. He knew what he had to do. He walked towards the ship without hesitation. Once inside the control cabin, he looked at the main screen. His destination was marked in the middle. The blue planet.

#

"Mr. President," the chief of staff hesitated for a moment. He knew the President was in an important meeting with the defense secretary and a few other generals. But he had no choice. The call was from Roland Graham, the only survivor on Mars.

"Mr. President, an urgent call from Mr. Graham," said the chief of staff.

"What now? Hasn't he departed the planet yet?" asked the President, looking at the others in the room. "Connect it."

The speaker crackled, and Rolland's face appeared on the screen.

"Mr. President, I have bad news for you. You must tighten your security. Whatever you have against extra-terrestrials. Right now."

"What...? What are you talking about?" the President barked. He saw the frightened faces of his generals as well.

"Mr. President, my return was not an anomaly. My ship had been redirected purposefully. By whom? I don't know. And the disease? My best guess is it was planted on me. To destroy the human population. I know this is wild...," Roland continued.

The President was already on his feet. Generals around the table were whispering to each other.

"Okay. Mr. Graham, you need to be more specific. Tell me what you know." The President adjusted his tie and sat again. He knew good leaders do not panic in situations like this.

Roland described how he deduced the possibility of an alien attack. Before launching the ship, he wanted to check one thing. The SP25-00 carried a time capsule. Like the first ancestors of it, the voyagers. A universal message to extra-terrestrial life forms out in the universe. The difference is the black box, as it was called at the time, had information preserved in all available storage techniques. From engraved gold plates to silicon chips. As he suspected, the black box was missing. It was attached to the base of the sleeping pod of its only passenger. He knew that Deon or any other at the company did not extract it. Suddenly, he realized what must have happened.

The distant memory of an incident inside the ship was not a dream. Someone had entered the vessel. Those who were in black uniforms. Short, stocky people with pale skin and yellow eyes. They directed the spacecraft toward Earth. To send a message.

Inside the empty cabin of the black box was a note. Engraved on a thin gold sheet.

"We are coming."

#

Dan Chimsky

Back To The Surface

Dan Chimsky

The horizontal movement of the wagon slowly stopped. A low mechanical sound replaced the hum of the motors. The side doors started to open. The ears were filled with a loud noise. And an unbearable stench materialized. Peter could not bring his hands to the nose or the ears fast enough. Inside the body bag, the space was limited. Barely enough for a motionless, dead body. Those were not designed for a living human to do acrobatics.

In the next moment, Peter felt the change in gravitational force. And his body started to slide. He had no option. But to glide with other heavy sacks. Some were already over his. He felt the pressure on his body parts increases.

"What the fuck is going on?" Alan, his partner, shouted from somewhere. Inside another bag.

"Shhh...," Peter tried to silence him unsuccessfully. There was no point in shushing over the excruciating noise.

In a few seconds, the rolling was over. Peter's legs were buried. The weight on his lower body was unbearable. Fortunately, his head was above the mass. And part of his upper body was not in the grip. He waited a few minutes. To make sure the transport carrier was gone. But he could not hear its engines as the constant clangor did not stop.

Peter managed to bring his hands over the weight of the other bags. He dragged the zipper with some effort. Finally, he peeked out.

"What the fuck?" He could not believe his eyes. More so, what they were sitting on. It was a massive heap of human bodies. All dead. And in various stages of decomposing. Most were still wrapped in tattered plastic body bags. Only the newly dumped loads were intact.

In every direction, he saw only the rotten flesh of human bodies. Then, Peter saw a motion to his left. That was Alan struggling to open the zipper of his bag.

"What the heck? This is disgusting," said Alan, comically trying to close his nose and ears simultaneously.

The air was heavy with an unbearable reek. The smell of decomposing flesh. And the agonizing sound continued over their heads.

The two teenagers were in a sizable chamber with a low-hanging roof. The ceiling was supported by a series of columns located at regular intervals. It was similar to the large convention halls in the underground community geodes. But much bigger.

Rotten human bodies were everywhere, in every direction, obscuring their view of the sidewalls. Only the wide strip in the middle was free. Somewhat.

The duo struggled to free themselves from body bags. Finally, Peter reached the maglev strip, jumping over the dead.

"What the hell is that noise?" Alan joined his friend.

"Don't know... Probably an air circulation fan. There should be an elevator shaft close by," Peter suggested.

"This must be the so-called cemetery geode. Let's follow the sound... It should be coming from the shaft connecting the surface."

Peter and Alan have never been to the earth's surface. None of the other humans, as far as they know. They had seen some centuries-old photos. Vast open areas with trees under the blue sky. A magical scene. But first, they should find a way out from here.

"Those fans shouldn't be this loud. This is unbearable," Alan tried to talk over the noise. "Did you notice? This is not uniform like a fan."

"Probably an old one."

According to history lessons at school, once humans lived on the earth's surface. Three hundred years ago, to be exact. Then, the outer world became inhabitable because of extreme weather patterns and high temperatures. With no other option, humans created geodes, the underground habitats that can harbor all of humanity.

Geodes are interconnected and located at least two to three hundred meters below the surface, deep inside the bedrock. Only connections to the surface are through elevator shafts that act as air intakes and transportation tunnels. No one knows what kind of stuff is transported to and from the surface. The elevator shafts are highly protected by the armed forces of the regime. No ordinary person ever entered an elevator shaft and came back alive.

"Don't think it is wise to stay here. Let's follow the tracks," said Peter.

"We don't know where it goes."

"We don't know about anything here. I think these tracks loop and go back to the elevator shaft."

"There could be guards and SpyCams," said Alan.

"Do we have any other option? Do you want to stay here with all these dead people?"

Alan dropped behind Peter. Both felt a strong breeze on their jackets. Something they had never experienced inside their community geode.

"Are those nano-bots... see, hovering over those bodies?" Alan pointed toward dead bodies. Then, Peter noticed the swarm, too.

"Don't think so... Look at that. There must be millions of them."

"Oh... I know. I know what they are." Alan excitedly stepped off the tracks. "Those are flies. I saw some photos of them. Remember the files we hacked from the museum? They are living animals... the same as us."

Most geode-living humans had never seen other animals. In the highly controlled underground environment, no other creatures are allowed. Ordinary people do not have access to farms. Those are separate geodes far from communities. And fully controlled remotely with minimum human involvement.

Information circulation in every community is managed and monitored by the regime. People know what is provided by the authorities. No additional information. Since its inception, the Movement has been trying to steal data from the government. Unfortunately, the info-net was unbreakable. The Movement is especially after the reports on the surface environment, past or present. So far, they have managed to acquire very little knowledge.

"I think the Movement is right. The regime lies about everything. One big lie is right here... in front of us. All these dead bodies. These are supposed to be deposited in a cemetery with dignity... not thrown like this. What is this? Where is the respect for the dead?" Peter's face was getting red, with bursting anger.

"Do you know what Uncle Brandon told me? The first generation had opposed making compost out of dead bodies. And they didn't want to incinerate inside the living geode either. So, they decided to establish cemetery geodes somewhere closer to the communities," Alan said, recalling the conversation with his uncle. "Relatives could visit those in the past. Access restriction is a new thing."

Recently, Peter and Alan learned about the process of dealing with the dead from a worker at the mortuary. They met

Liam during an illegal gathering and quickly became friends. According to him, the dead bodies are transported to a geode closer to the surface, not near the community. He had never seen the complete process. But knew some details. Fast decomposition needs proper temperature and humidity. However, it needs a higher energy demand. The easiest way was to establish cemetery geodes closer to the surface. Where energy demands are lower. Liam suggested traveling on the disposal train to the cemetery first. Then, it would be easier to access the top from there.

"This is what they are doing... disgusting idiots. Probably, we are already on the surface. That is where these other animals live somehow. The regime lied about that, too."

"Yes... but how do they keep this a secret for so long?" asked Alan.

"It is simple... The regime controls everything. No one has access to the surface. Or to the restricted sections of the info-net. I'm sure only a few big guys at the top know about these. The people in the central Geode... and the Governor's office."

Suddenly, Peter noticed a movement behind dead bodies to his left. Something big. Could there be other types of animals? Animals bigger than flies. And more dangerous creatures. The thought sent a chill along his spine.

"What the hell is that?" asked Alan. "Something big. That looks like a dog. But that is not a dog."

The regime allowed some dogs as pets inside community geodes, but only for some chosen families... rich and powerful. Both had seen a few dogs at the central park.

"What the fuck... They are eating dead bodies," said Peter, realizing the danger. "Don't think they understand the difference between living and dead humans. See... there are more in the back."

The lights above the tracks did not illuminate the far side. More animals started to appear among dead bodies.

"I think they are afraid of the train. Once it is gone, they come to feast from the new dump," said Peter.

One of the rodents, one larger than the others, raised its head. And looked at the two moving bodies. Sniffed the air and opened its mouth. But the duo didn't hear anything over the sound of the wind. Suddenly, hundreds of other animals appeared behind piles of carcasses. The animals were aimed towards the tracks.

"That doesn't look good... move faster," Peter shouted to Alan.

The slow walk became a jog. More animals appeared from all sides. Jog became a run. Soon, they were running as fast as they could.

#

With attention towards the scurrying animals, Peter or Alan didn't notice when they passed a partitioning wall. They had entered another large chamber similar to the previous one. Suddenly, it occurred to them. There were no decomposing bodies. But millions of bones. As far as they could see. No flies. No big animals. Except for the few still chasing them along the tracks now.

"I think this is a previous dumping ground. Those animals must have cleaned them up." Peter slowed down. Then, he looked over his shoulder to check the progress of their pursuers. He noticed the wall separating two chambers and a large entrance in the middle. Large enough to let the train pass through on the tracks. A few animals were still following them, but cautiously and slowly.

"Look at that... I think a staircase," Alan pointed in the opposite direction.

They could see the far walls of the chamber. As the flesh was decomposed, the piles of bones were not high enough to cover the walls. The lights along the track reached far and reflected on white bones. They were in a massive windowless chamber. The tracks bisected it in the middle. There was an entrance that looked like a staircase at the far end of the hall.

Peter realized that the sound of the wind was coming through the stairwell. He looked back and saw the closing animals. Now, a little faster and with renewed numbers. The two had only one option.

The lights on the ceiling started to dim. Peter and Alan managed to reach the staircase before it went completely dark. Peter took a flashlight from his pant pockets and aimed upwards. They climbed up. The sound of the wind got louder.

The youngsters were sweating inside their jackets. Knowing it would be much colder in the mortuary, where they were hidden for several hours, the two came prepared with an additional layer. But the new environment is entirely different and something they never expected. More humid and wet than they have ever experienced.

Peter and Alan climbed several levels, passing large chambers. All those were like the one they arrived. They didn't bother to check what's inside those. All were in the same condition. No signs of humans, alive or dead.

A faint light appeared above them. And the sound got louder as they climbed up. The wind started to get stronger. After laboring steps for several minutes, they arrived in an open space. But, unlike in lower levels, there were no walls. They could see beyond the chamber. The lights came from every direction. Not from the equipment on the ceiling.

The two boys were in the middle of a building, barely managing to stand still. Strong winds swept between the floor and the roof. Fast-moving water drops hit their faces like needles. They looked at each other, not understanding what they were seeing. Peter walked towards the edge of the floor against the wind. Alan followed him.

"This is it?" Alan had to shout over the roaring wind.

"Yes... We are on the surface," Peter yelled.

The two watched the surroundings with awe. They could see a dark grey sky between buildings of various heights around them, as far as they could see. All were in a similarly dilapidated condition. Water poured from the sky on the structures. The wind roared through buildings.

Suddenly, a bright white streak appeared in the sky, blinding their eyes. It started out of nowhere and ended on top of a tall building. Within seconds, both crouched, shivering. The thunderous sound had such effect they hunkered involuntarily. The two youngsters were frightened, not understanding any of these. They ran towards the staircase again.

The two realized there were more levels above. But they were afraid to face unknown dangers. They had no protection against strong winds, falling water drops, or weird light streaks and sounds. Peter dragged Alan and ran down. They stopped one level below and sat close to each other on the stairs, looking at the empty chamber, fearing flesh-eating animals would arrive there.

#

"Now, I remember what that is," said Alan, looking at his partner. "It is called a storm. That brings down water from the sky and strong winds. The lights and sounds are called lightning and thundering. ...something to do with electric charges between the ground and the sky. I didn't understand that part. This was one of the reasons humans abandoned living on the surface. Before that, it used to be a calm climate everywhere. Nothing like this... but, lately, storms like this became frequent."

"That's interesting... hard to believe scientists at the time did not have a solution ...other than going underground," said Peter.

"How can someone live with this wind? And with water pouring from the sky like this? ...these storms must have flooded the communities. I think we are in one of those cities. You saw those buildings... only the stronger sections remain after all these years. Lower levels are somehow saved because they are located underground. This could be a minor storm... who knows."

Lightning illuminated the lower level through the stairwell. They noticed the increased frequency of thundering.

"I think we are just one level below the ground. How many are down there? ...six or seven levels? The tracks are at the lowest level, I guess. The entrance to the elevator shaft should be there," said Peter.

"We didn't see anything on our way," reminded Alan. There were no windows in the train wagon. And they were zippered in body bags. "Could there be guards at the entrance?"

"I don't think so. Everything must be automated. No reason to have guards here... there are no people on the surface."

"That's true. The regime wants to stop people moving out of the geodes... not coming in," said Alan, observing the empty chamber. "Do you think anyone else participated in the event?"

Someone who recently joined the Movement proposed the idea of the 'Back to the Surface' event. It was organized as an act of revolution against the regime. However, the information was not entered into the info-net to avoid the keen eyes of the authorities. The event details were shared as printed material. And only among trusted members. An old method used by humans centuries ago. It was a slow process, especially between geodes. Only a very few had the privilege to travel to another community. Peter and Alan received a pamphlet from a good friend who works closely with the Movement.

The members of the Movement believe the surface is still habitable. However, according to the regime, the surface is unsuitable for humans. There are minimal operations, such as extracting valuable minerals on the surface. All those activities are carried out by automated machines.

The Movement members believe the regime restricts surface access to control the citizens. People cannot move between geodes without permission from the respective authorities. Humans do not like to stay in one place. The unrest among people has been rising, although not shown in public.

In such background, the Movement was initiated in the central geode. It slowly established across peripheral communities. Because of the travel restrictions, information flow was limited and slow. However, the members managed to infiltrate data repositories controlled by the regime. The files smuggled so far had valuable information on the history and current conditions of the surface. The newly acquired knowledge was carefully disseminated among trusted members. However, efforts to create opposition against the regime were not successful. Therefore, only a small group, mainly young people, were happy to join the Movement.

Although they organized the back-to-the-surface event with the utmost secrecy, the regime was ahead of the Movement. A few leaders in the central geode were arrested. Last-minute warnings in the info-net discouraged many members willing to join the event.

"There are only two other elevator shafts from our geode. Those are highly guarded. We could be the only two from ours," said Peter.

"If anyone from other geodes managed to arrive on the surface, they must arrive far from here. The closest geode to ours is NA2011. How far is it? ...ten kilometers straight? We don't know where they emerged on the surface. Even if someone arrived, they would take a long time to find us. Without our WDAs, there is no way to contact anyone." Alan looked at his empty wrist.

The two didn't carry their wearable digital assistants, commonly known as WDAs. They knew that the regime monitors every individual through WDAs. Also, they were uncertain about the functionality of the units beyond the geodes, especially at the surface.

"I'm pretty sure at least some members from the central geode must have arrived on the surface," said Peter.

"I don't think the regime expected anyone to take the lead. That was a massive campaign against the event for the last few days... no one would be brave enough to participate. But I don't think they expected anyone would go in body bags." Alan said with a smile on his face.

Once they learned about the back-to-the-surface event, Peter and Alan planned to recruit some close friends. No one was interested. Or they were afraid to break the law. Peter proposed to hide in the mortuary and sneaked into a disposal wagon disguised as a dead body.

Mortuary is a fully automated facility. The security at the facility was minimal. The transport carrier takes dead bodies to a cemetery geode once they have enough numbers, which is very frequent for a medium-sized geode like theirs. Alan hacked into the data system of the mortuary with some help from Liam. There are only two human workers, including

Liam, at the facility. He helped Alan to erase logging data and turned off monitoring cameras for one hour. That was enough for them to enter the facility without authorization and get into a carrier with other dead people.

The central geode is the largest of all, with approximately ten million people living in it. Naturally, the regime has its headquarters in the central geode. In the beginning, the Movement was not strong and had several factions. But slowly started to amalgamate and spread towards other smaller geodes. Some communities farthest from the central geode are believed to have better-organized chapters of the Movement. Those smaller geodes were designed to keep a maximum of one million people. Hence, the regime keeps the absolute minimum force to control the inhabitants.

"Okay, what do we do now? No doubt, we are the only two on the surface now. Even if someone else arrived from another geode, we won't find them," said Alan.

"We are on the surface anyway. We should explore a little more," Peter suggested.

"We have very little food... maybe for two or three days. And no guns. I don't like those nasty animals."

"Agree... We should have researched more. Didn't expect to see animals up here. Who knows?" said Peter, standing from the staircase. "Let's find something to scare those animals."

"First, we should find the entrance to the elevator shaft. Then we can come back to explore."

"We know where to find the train tracks. I'm sure... we can jump back into the carrier when it dumps body bags next time."

"Let's go down again, then. We'll follow the tracks. I think they've been filling the chambers from this side."

The duo climbed down into the darkness. Peter carried the flashlight. Both tried to pay attention to any movement, fearing flesh-eating rodents. They could not hear any noise coming from lower levels. The continuous sound of thundering was unbearable. The uproar of wind sweeping through the upper floors of the building masked any other sound.

They arrived at the lowest level without any incident. Peter aimed his flashlight towards the left, the chamber full of fresh dead bodies. There was no sign of rodents. Alan picked a bone, a long human thigh bone, from the pile of bones.

Better be prepared against the animals. They turned right and followed the tracks. It was completely dark except for the beam of the flashlight.

The two entered a tunnel, which is familiar to geode-living teenagers. The communities are connected to several smaller service geodes by tunnels. Peter examined the ceiling for any cameras. There was none. Instead, he noticed light fixtures along the midline.

"It is an automated system. Lights are switched on when the carrier is here." Alan suggested.

"No need to waste energy for dead people."

Geothermal energy is the only energy source available for geode communities. Although there was no shortage, the regime strictly controls electricity grids.

#

Peter and Alan arrived in another large chamber. It was full of automobiles covered in a thick layer of dust. Parked neatly in rows. Those were large and in many different sizes and shapes. Unlike the small EVs, they see in their geode.

"These must be the vehicles people used three hundred years ago," said Peter, approaching one of the big trucks.

"I've read about these automobiles. Apparently, they had used hydrocarbon oil to run the motors of these. They extracted oil from the ground... like we excavate minerals in extraction geodes. The article suggested the combustion of hydrocarbon oils was the main reason for air pollution. People have switched to different energy sources in the last two centuries of surface living. But it was too late."

"So, the regime is right about the surface environment?"

"It is not only the pollution. Those pollutants contributed to something called global warming. The surface was once several degrees cooler than now. But those pollutants contributed to warming the planet. So, it became intolerable for humans and animals. There was a large-scale extinction of other species... both plants and animals... even before humans started to go underground."

Suddenly, Peter stopped and switched off his flashlight.

"What is..."

"Shh..."

They were in the dark. Nothing was moving. No sounds except the noisy wind above them. Alan tightened his grip on the bone.

"Did you see that?" Peter whispered.

"What?" Alan stepped closer to his friend.

"Look... I saw a light ahead of us. Like a flashlight."

"Could that be another staircase? Maybe lightning from the storm."

"No, it was more like a torch light... moving."

"The guards?"

Staying in the middle of the tracks is not a good idea. Especially if guards are coming. Peter dragged his friend towards the closest row of machines. Quickly, both crouched behind a big truck. And stayed behind the vehicle for almost five minutes. No sign of anyone.

For a moment, Peter thought that it could be the lightning. Penetrated through a stairwell. He was about to stand up. Then, they saw it again. A faint light. At the far corner of the track, where it seems to bend.

"Did you see that?" Peter whispered again.

"Yeah... looks like someone is coming this way along the tracks."

The two sat there for a little longer to confirm what was coming. The flashlight appeared frequently. There were at least two light beams. A group of people was coming along a tunnel towards the chamber.

"What do we do now? They are coming this way. It could be a search party," said Alan. The lights emerged from the tunnel. Now, on the straight run of the tracks.

"Three guards!"

Peter and Alan could see the silhouettes of three human shapes. Reflection of their flashlights on dirty walls and automobiles barely illuminated moving men. But it was enough to reveal the details of three tall men.

"Who are they? They are not regime guards," said Alan.

"We better move away from the tracks," Peter suggested. "They'll be on us in a few minutes."

Peter crawled away from the midline, passing several rows of vehicles. Alan followed on his knees, moving towards the far wall. It was completely dark in the back. But the two moved. The flashlights of the visitors were still in the far.

Peter and Alan stopped behind a large, square-shaped automobile. It had massive wheels, wide enough to hide the two youngsters behind one. Peter couldn't hear the footsteps of intruders. But the flashlights came closer and closer. The visitors were on a predictable path.

#

The two boys were sitting behind the wheel with a deflated tire. The flashlights danced along the tracks. And stopped where they were crouched a few minutes ago. The visitors aimed their beams between rows of vehicles. They were indeed searching for someone.

Peter quickly realized the mistake they made. He was mad at himself for ignoring the obvious. One flashlight aimed between the two rows of vehicles they crawled a moment ago. The disturbance in the thick layer of dust was unmistakable. Their crawling knee marks.

The light beam moved away from the markings on the floor and towards the tracks again. Peter and Alan stayed silent, hugging their knees. It felt like an eternity. They could feel their own heartbeats thumping loudly. Both tried to listen for footsteps without any success. The wind noise masked all other audible sounds. They were not sure whether those men moved along the tracks. Or they were still there. There was a faint light, but it was not moving.

Suddenly, everything became blinding white in front of their eyes. The duo tried to see through the sputtering eyelids. Two powerful light beams were staring at them. Peter and Alan attempted to cover it with their palms unsuccessfully. They couldn't see anything against the lights. Peter realized what had just happened. The three men had come around the vehicle without the aid of their flashlights. Apparently, the visitors knew how to navigate in the dark. This is their territory, after all.

"Who are you?" a deep voice behind the lights asked.

Peter and Alan noticed a long metal object with a sharp end aimed at them. Something they haven't seen before. One guy kicked the thigh bone beside Alan. It disappeared underneath the vehicle.

"We... we lost our way," said Peter.

The third guy, standing behind the other two, switched on a red light. The lantern illuminated a small circular area around them. And created long shadows on the walls behind standing men. The other two switched off their flashlights.

Three tall men. Taller than anyone Peter and Alan had seen in their lifetime. They noticed the dark skin of the three visitors. Another first for two boys. Although they learned about people of darker skin colors, they had never seen such people until now. They knew that people of color lived in separate smaller geodes far from the central and other mega geodes.

The clothes were not like the outfits of the regime guards. And were different from each other. Not a uniform.

"On your knees... Hands behind head," ordered the tallest of the three, now in the middle. "Why did you come here?"

"We are from the NA 2012 geode. We came in the disposal train a little while ago. We can't find our way back," said Peter.

"Ha... earthworms," said the guy with a scarred face. Peter noticed a faint smile. The scar across his face was more noticeable against the low light of the lantern.

"Could be a trap. Guards must be somewhere around. They must have started to hunt humans again." The shortest of the three looked at the man in the middle, clearly their leader.

The leader pointed his weapon at Peter's chest.

"Toss your bags here," said the captain while signaling the Scarface. The guy opened two backpacks and unloaded everything on the dusty floor. There were two more flashlights, first aid kits, and pre-packaged emergency food and water packs. Nothing else. Looking at the pile, Peter realized how ill-prepared they were for an excursion like this. Not even extra clothes. The Scarface moved the items on the floor using his weapon.

"Ha... beggars," Scarface had a sarcastic smile on his lips.

The leader signaled to Peter. "Stand up... take off your jacket."

Peter dropped his jacket on the floor. Scarface checked his body and his pant pockets.

"Where's your WDA?" asked the leader.

"We didn't bring those."

The leader signaled Peter to kneel again. They followed the same procedure for Alan. Finally, the three men were satisfied.

"Why did you come here?" asked the leader.

"Do you live on the surface?" Peter couldn't contain himself.

"Answer the question," Scarface shouted.

"We didn't expect anyone to live on the surface. That's what we were taught. We wanted to explore it and look for ourselves." The leader didn't show any expression. Peter decided not to reveal about the 'Back to the surface' event. And about the Movement, at least for now.

"We believed the surface could still be habitable... wanted to check that," Alan said.

"You both are fools. This is not a fun field trip for earthworms," said Scarface.

The leader asked them to stand and pick up their belongings. Once they packed their backpacks, he ordered them to walk towards the tracks. Peter and Alan followed the leader. The other two were on their flanks with weapons ready.

No escape now. Trying to escape these people in an unknown environment could be suicidal.

All of them walked silently along the tracks toward the tunnel. There were two large sacks leaning against the wall at the entrance. Peter and Alan noticed blood on the floor. And on the sacks as well. Peter realized what was inside when the shorter guy rearranged the stuff in his bag. Dead rodents. The leader helped the two guys to pick up their load. They balanced the bags on their broad shoulders.

After two more chambers and connecting tunnels, they deviated from the path of the tracks. The group passed several other similar halls and tunnels before entering a staircase. Unlike the first one, Peter and Alan climbed to the surface an hour ago, the walls of this staircase had drawings. Words and figures didn't look ancient. Or familiar. Peter was sure these were works of people living on the surface now.

A faint light appeared above, at the top of the stairwell. And the sounds of the storm were louder. After climbing a few levels, instead of going up, they turned. And went through another tunnel. It was illuminated by light fixtures hanging from its ceiling. The difference was noticeable. Those were different from the ones they saw along the tracks. Low illumination and ancient looking.

The group walked for another few minutes. Then, they arrived in a long and narrow hall. The entrance was barricaded with a metal gate.

The people behind the gate were somehow aware of the approach of this new group. All black faces, the same as the other three, looked at the two ghostly white teenagers. Most were armed with weapons Peter and Alan had not seen before. They all wore camouflaged uniforms, but not like the black outfits of the regime guards. One person talked to the leader of the group. Peter couldn't understand what they were discussing. A different language.

#

Two armed guards directed two boys to walk with them. The leader of the hunting party followed them, now without his weapon. The other two disappeared behind a door with their heavy bags.

After a series of turns and walks along illuminated corridors, the group stopped at a large wooden door. Peter read the little square sign on the door.

Colonel Keisha Santos. Division Commander.

One of the guards knocked before entering the room. A woman was sitting behind a large office table. The wall behind her was covered with an enormous map. She was dressed in a camouflaged uniform as of the guards. But with more decorations on her chest and upper arms. Peter and Alan could not hide their surprise. They have never heard of female leaders in any of the underground communities.

The guard who opened the door introduced the leader of the hunting party, Obiad Olonga.

"Please, have a seat." The colonel signaled them to sit. Olonga and two boys sat on the chairs in front of the table. The two guards remained standing behind Peter and Alan.

"What is this about?" She asked, examining the youngsters.

"We were hunting along the train tracks. Found these boys hiding in the base level parking garage... of tower three.

They say they are from the geode and wanted to explore the surface," explained Olonga.

The colonel silently watched the two young faces.

"So, you want to explore the earth?" She had a faint smile on her face.

"Yes, we were always taught that the surface is inhabitable. Because of the dangers up here, the government controls access to the top. We doubted it. Recently, we learned more about the surface environment. So, we thought it could not be as dangerous as they teach. We wanted to check it ourselves," said Peter, repeating their earlier version to Olonga. Keisha listened carefully.

"How did you escape the guards?"

"We knew that the cemetery geode is located closer to the surface. So, we came in a transport carrier... disguised as dead bodies. There are no guards at the mortuary. We managed to get on the train without any trouble. Our plan was to find an elevator shaft to the top."

Peter had seen enough to understand the difference. The colonel doesn't fit in anywhere in the regime government. He remembered what one of the hunters said about the guards. The regime used to kill humans on the surface.

Still, Peter didn't want to make any assumptions. What if these people have some connections with the regime? Suddenly, it clicked in his mind, something he didn't realize earlier. Olonga, the leader of the hunting party, asked about their WDAs. How do they know about WDAs? Do they know more about the people living down, or have they had someone from below earlier? Peter didn't want to rule out anything yet. He thought to be cautious and keep details about the Movement a secret, at least for now.

"What made you think the surface is habitable?" The colonel asked Alan, who stayed silent so far.

"Everyone says the surface is unsuitable for living because of storms and flooding. And we can't tolerate high temperatures on the surface. But three hundred years is a long period. We thought that conditions must have changed after all these years," Alan replied.

"Who told you that it might be different now? Are there others who think like you?"

Peter was hesitant. Alan looked at Peter.

"Yes, most students discuss this in our schools. But we don't have access to data," said Peter.

"Did they teach you how the earth became inhabitable?"

"We learned about the global warming effect... started hundreds of years ago. A usual cyclic event, but it was extreme in the current cycle," Alan said.

"Is that all?" They noticed the frustrated look on her face. She looked at her guards. And shook her head.

"Haven't they ever taught you that humans destroyed the earth?" the colonel asked. Peter and Alan looked at each other.

"Some people believe that is the case. But no one knows for sure. We don't have information other than what is available in the info-net," said Alan.

Another woman in uniform who was much younger than the leader entered the room from a side door. She placed three glasses in front of the visitors. The colonel thanked her and signaled them to drink. Peter realized how thirsty he was when he saw the glasses. They did not drink anything for the last five hours. Peter and Alan drained their glasses at once. Something they had never tasted. But pleasantly sweet.

"We know what's going on down there. We have a system in place to monitor developments in the geodes," said the colonel. Peter and Alan looked at each other.

"You work with the regime?" asked Alan.

"No, we do not. We value the freedom of individuals. Whether they live underground or on the surface. The regime left millions of people on the surface to die when they decided to go underground. That's three hundred years ago. But we survived. Humans are resilient. We adapted to new conditions. Not to mention, we had many difficulties on the surface. But we are working to make the earth a better place again," she said.

"But... but," Peter had many questions to ask.

"This is Amaya," the colonel cut off Peter and pointed to the young woman. She was obediently standing beside her leader.

"She will take you to your quarters... and to the places you must see. Hope this storm will end soon. If so, you might be able to go outside. Once you learn about the earth, you can decide what to do next. Don't try to escape. There are many dangers outside. You will not survive a day without our assistance. You understand?" The colonel warned, carefully examining two faces.

Peter and Alan knew the conversation was over. They had more questions, but those had to wait. They were not sure whether they were under arrest or not. Amaya asked them to come with her. There was no other choice. Other than to follow her.

#

"I think we can go out tomorrow," Amaya gestured towards the sky.

"How do you predict that?" asked Alan.

They were standing on the topmost floor of a tall building. Thirty-eighth level, to be exact. Raindrops were intermittent. And no strong wind across the building, as they experienced the last time. There was no lightning or thunder. The scene of tall towers against the grey sky was astonishing. There were buildings as far as they could see.

"See... the wind is not strong anymore. Clouds are getting thinner. They are more whitish now. You might see the sun soon."

Peter and Alan were delighted, like two kids in a candy store. This is the first time in their life they are going to see the sun. Not to mention, everything they saw in the last two days was new.

After the meeting with the division commander, Amaya arranged everything for Peter and Alan. A guest room with two beds for sleeping. She showed them a place to eat. A canteen closer to their accommodation. A large community hall where food is served three times a day. Uniformed men and women came to eat every day at the right time. Well disciplined. None of them were white-skinned. They all looked at these two strange-looking boys. Some even talked with them. They all were friendly and welcoming.

Amaya took the two youngsters around to show them the surroundings. People were living underground. As Amaya called them, the base levels of abandoned tall buildings. Those were built hundreds of years ago. That was before the geodes were built. But the connecting tunnels between buildings were new. Once overland movements became impossible because of storms and flooding, the only option was to go underground.

"This is more like where we live," suggested Peter.

"Except, we live three hundred meters below the surface." Alan agreed.

People had everything they needed at these base levels. The greenhouses for growing food plants. And shelters for animals. All Peter and Alan had never seen. They observed large animals named cows for the first time, with amazement. They could not believe it when Amaya said the drinks they had been drinking in the mornings were from these animals.

On their way to the top level, they observed energy production units. Upper levels of the building were fitted with rows of fans along the edge. The fans were massive and extended from floor to ceiling.

"The wind is the only energy source we have. It is a good one... It doesn't harm the environment," said Amaya. The two boys observed the fans rotating at a steady speed.

"Once your ancestors abandoned living on the surface, remaining people converted these buildings for energy production. We are on a stormy planet. So, there is no shortage of wind. Low-cost energy."

"Is it like this every day?" Peter pointed to the sky.

"Almost... We have storms regularly... roughly every three weeks. And it can last up to ten to twelve days. You can imagine how much rain we get from these storms. We have walls around these towers to avoid flooding in base levels. In a lucky year, we might see the sun for a maximum of ten to fifteen days. Otherwise, it is always cloudy."

"Oh, that is why everywhere is so wet," said Peter.

"You see all those green?" Amaya pointed towards the ceiling. "Moss... that is a living organism like plants. Those grow everywhere, even with low light conditions." The two boys realized why all the other towers seemed greenish.

"Is it hot like this every day?" asked Alan.

"Yeah... you feel hot because of high humidity. You know... it used to be cold in some months. But we don't get snow anymore. Not even in the north, I guess."

"What is snow?"

"Oh, that happens when the temperature goes below zero degrees. Instead of raindrops, powdery stuff called snow falls from the sky. But we haven't had such an event for the last hundred years."

"We never thought the surface environment is this complicated," Peter said.

"I will show you some photos and videos from the last snowfall. Stunning... like a magical land. Sadly, we don't see it anymore. Because nowhere on earth have sub-zero temperatures."

They walked back towards the staircase. All three sat down on the stairs and shared some snacks they brought. Much needed rest for the inexperienced boys. Climbing thirty-eight floors was not an easy task.

Meanwhile, Amaya explained weather patterns on the surface. This information was like a fairy tale for geode-living teenagers.

"We didn't see anyone like us," Peter changed the subject. "I mean white skin like ours." A question he had since their arrival.

"That goes back to the origin of your underground living," said Amaya. "Early scientists experimented with underground geodes or similar structures. That was a long time ago. In fact, long ago, there were underground transport systems for several centuries. Mostly, closer to the surface, though. When the earth became inhabitable, the government decided to go underground. But there was a problem. There was not enough space and facilities for everyone. Solution? They allowed only the selected groups."

"That's cruel. So, some people had to stay up here?" asked Alan.

"Yes, most of the white people got the opportunity. They left the others on the surface. But people lived for about another century, obviously with many difficulties. Then, there was a long period of disasters. The environment changed rapidly. Massive storms as never seen before and continuous flooding. And extreme heat events in between. The sea level rose really quickly. The worst was the new diseases that spread fast among communities. That lasted for around fifty years. Billions of people died all over the world. We lost all communication systems across the world. And power generation units. That was a total disaster. Humans were almost wiped out from the earth's surface. And many other animals and plants as well. By that time, the regime was in full control down there. They didn't do anything to save the remaining humans on the surface. Geodes were self-sustainable. They didn't need anything from the surface except for air."

A complete shocker. Peter and Alan knew nothing about this. Both felt guilty. Even though they had nothing to do with the acts of their ancestors or the regime.

"Survivors of that disastrous period were people like us. Those who had origins in the tropical regions. For some reason, they had better immunity. People with the genetic capacity to evolve resistance against diseases survived, and others did not. But there are still people like you elsewhere... but not many." Amaya explained.

"This was once called New York. At its peak, it had nearly fifteen million people. One of the biggest at the time. Look at all those buildings. Now we have barely a half a million in the whole region," Amaya said, looking around. "There are other cities like this all over the continent. The total population on the earth's surface does not exceed fifty million now."

"Are there other places, too?" asked Alan, surprised by this new information.

"Oh, yeah... Everywhere. But only small groups of people. Most of the tropical areas are flooded now... because of the increasing sea levels. But there are people in the remaining highlands and former temperate regions like here. Only some have enough technology to contact with each other."

"Do you have contacts with them? Can you go to other places?" Peter asked. She shook her head.

"Travel is impossible on the land. First, there is no proper road network now. And we get only a short window, probably about four weeks in July and August, without strong storms. That's the only time we can travel overland. But we still have some sections of the old subterranean tunnel system... built five hundred years ago. Unfortunately, your regime destroyed a large chunk of that network."

"Oh... we're sorry," Alan said with a guilty feeling.

"No, it's not your fault. That happened centuries ago."

"How do you contact other groups then?" asked Peter.

"No travels. Crossing the ocean is beyond our capacity. We can't fight against the storms in the ocean." Amaya showed the sky between tall towers. It was still drizzling under gray clouds.

"When the regime established their power, they destroyed remaining satellites in outer space. Because they didn't need them... Or they couldn't maintain those from the geodes. We lost all means of communication between populations. Luckily, our ancestors managed to find a mechanism, a radio transmission system. Only a few hobbyists had practiced at the time. It's slow and sketchy, especially in bad weather."

Both Alan and Peter had more questions. Everything they learned from Amaya was new. They felt anger against the regime government. The two realized the importance of the Movement and its acts against the regime. Interestingly, Amaya knew about the Movement. And even about the Back to the Surface event.

They continued their discussion, exchanging information about their worlds. Hoping for the sun to appear among clouds.

#

"You have learned everything about the surface. And what the regime has done to innocent people here and the earth. It's up to you to decide. You can help humanity. Or you can go down and live there." Colonel Keisha Santos observed the faces of two youngsters. Peter and Alan were sitting in front of her. Amaya was obediently standing behind her superior.

Alan looked at his partner. And said, "We would like to stay here."

"You are always welcome. But... there is something else." The colonel looked at her subordinate. Amaya shook her head slightly.

"Have you ever seen a person with yellow eyes?" Keisha asked.

"No... why?" answered Alan right away.

Peter was puzzled by the question. Suddenly, he remembered.

"Our governor has... the governor of the geode. Why?"

"Can you describe him?"

"He is a short... little bulky man. Nothing unusual. But I remember he has pale yellowish eyes."

"Oh yes... His wife, too," Alan said.

"Here is what you all don't know. Your governor is an alien... someone from a different planet... from a different galaxy. In fact, we don't know where they came from. We assume they are from a faraway place in the universe."

"What? What does it even mean?" Alan looked at his partner. Peter had an open mouth and wide eyes.

"I know... it is hard to believe. Humans long believed there could be intelligent life in the universe. But never had concrete evidence for such aliens elsewhere." Keisha started to explain life beyond the solar system, beyond the Milky Way. The two boys listened as if it was a fairy tale. They saw stars for the first time only two nights ago.

"People speculated about alien visits for a long time. In fact, there were a few credible reports of such encounters around five hundred years ago. Then suddenly came the attack out of nowhere. That was when the earth was having trouble surviving... because of the environmental changes."

"So, they are not humans?" asked Peter.

"They are. But evolved somewhere else. We don't know the full story here. What we know is that they are technologically advanced. They easily captured the earth. Made alliances with some of our population. And took them underground."

"Are they the regime leaders in the central geode?" asked Peter.

"You got it. Not only the central geode... All underground communities. All the top positions are held by those aliens. That includes the regime forces. So, they control every aspect of life down there. You all are their subjects."

"Why don't they control you?" Alan asked.

"That's an interesting question. For some reason, they don't like the surface living. Otherwise, with their advanced technology, they could easily make arrangements for living up here. Our only explanation is that these aliens could be from a planet where the underground living was normal."

"But... but how do they go back?" Peter asked. "I mean to their earth... wherever it is."

"This is the interesting part. For some reason, this group lost contact with their mother planet. We don't know why. There is no more travel as far as we know."

"So, they are alone here?" asked Peter. Keisha nodded her head.

"You have a choice," she said, looking at the two boys.

"Now you know the full story. The regime is not what you think. We need to take our earth back. It's up to you to decide."

Peter and Alan looked at each other.

"We need you down there. That way, you can help us with that important task."

"How?" asked Peter.

"We have connections with the Movement. But they need to be more organized. They need more people like you. Also, we need information. You can easily do that." She examined their faces.

"There's another thing. We have enough reasons to believe the regime is planning another attack on humans on the surface. So, it is crucial to have more eyes and ears down there. You already helped us a lot by providing the latest information."

Peter involuntarily looked at Amaya. He realized that all their conversations with her were part of that exercise. It reminded him of how she tried to discuss every aspect of geode living. At the time, they thought it was just out of curiosity.

"Are they? ...Why? They have everything down there," said Peter.

"They don't want any living being out of their control. And the regime is eyeing for more resources on the surface. Also, when there is a war against someone, it is easy to control dissidents... like the Movement. An age-old tactic of dictators." Keisha explained.

Peter and Alan have seen enough. And heard enough about the cruelty of the regime. More importantly, about their origin. It was not difficult to decide.

"We like to live here. But we'll do whatever we can do." Peter looked at Alan.

"Yes, anything we can do," said Alan.

Both Amaya and the colonel smiled.

#

Dan Chimsky

Back to the Surface

Dan Chimsky

The Bone Box
Talking to dead with Benjamin Gibson

When Ben received a package early morning, he didn't expect it to be a dead body. A boxful of human bones. The dead man himself had arranged the delivery. The former drug lord has an unfinished task.

Ben is the only human who can see and talk to the dead. And help them to move on from the dreadful trap they are in. Unfortunately, most others die in the process of liberating these innocent spirits. The young man, who doesn't like harming others, is somehow entangled in the network of dead and criminals. Whether it is a serial killer or a greedy businessman, there's no escape from the wrath of the deceased. And from Benjamin Gibson.

These are stories of the dead and desperate souls. Dan Chimsky takes you through a journey of unfathomable human cravings.

Dan Chimsky